HOW TO BREAK BAD NEWS

Tim Molloy

Virgin Books
65 Bleecker Street, 6th floor
New York, New York 10012
www.virginbooksusa.com

Distributed by Macmillan

This is a work of fiction. All of the characters, companies, organizations,
and events are either the products of the author's imagination or are used
fictitiously and are not to be understood as real.

FIRST EDITION

Designed by Jason Snyder

Library of Congress Cataloging-in-Publication Data

Molloy, Tim.
 How to break bad news / by Tim Molloy. — 1st ed.
    p. cm.
 ISBN-13: 978-0-7535-1500-6
 ISBN-10: 0-7535-1500-8
 1. Journalists—Fiction. 2. Los Angeles (Calif.)—Fiction. 3. Man-woman
relationships—Fiction. I. Title.
 PS3613.O47H69 2008
 813'.6—dc22

                              2008009437

10 9 8 7 6 5 4 3 2 1

For Deeds

Acknowledgments

Thank you to the following people:

Devin McIntyre at Mary Evans, Inc., for his good humor about doing so much more than an agent should have to do.

Ken Siman for working so hard to see this through, and for his creativity and open-mindedness.

Devin Ness for having the generosity to say this was worth doing, and the diligence to do it.

My editor, Caroline Trefler, for making this better and convincing me to kill my not-so-darlings.

My copy editor, Ann Espuelas, for her improvements, repairs, and protection of two languages.

And all the good people at Virgin Books.

My classmates at UCLA writing workshops, and my teachers: Claire Carmichael, Maureen Connell, Seth Greenland, and especially Mark Haskell Smith, who did as much as anyone to make this book happen.

Julie Buxbaum for her early reads and generous help.

Juan Carlos Montoya for his feedback, best frienditude, and technical advice on clown dancing.

Vince Gonzales, for explaining how he does some of his magic. Lisa Sweetingham, for risking her good name to help this along.

My family, for their love and support, and for letting me skip soccer practice. The members of a certain hip-hop-and-vigor-stick-obsessed secret society. The celebrated New York City improv group Orphan Tycoon.

Bobby Moynihan, one of the many from whom Frank stole.

And, most important, Deirdre McCarrick, my first editor, special lady, and rivuh companion. Thank you for making me a better writer and a better person.

LOS ANGELES, Nov. 11 I think of the rapper, shot in the back, and try to remember I'm lucky.

The jury acquitted the country ingénue of killing him after reviewing the video of their duet at the Concert for Traditional Marriage. The intensity of the rapper's krumping, more than his sudden removal of her chaps in front of millions of television viewers, convinced them she opened fire backstage only in self-defense. Now she was free to make the talk-show rounds, warning other women about the evils of clown dancing.

Red state, blue state, sex, race, death. It was this year's trial of the century and as reporters we had to be there. Neglecting, some of us, people we love for the length of the dirty summer.

Bad as it was, it could have been so much worse. I try to remember I'm lucky, luckier than 99 percent of the people in the world—except the ones who weren't dumped last night by the girl they wanted to marry.

"Don't fall in," Rich says, tugging me back and pointing too obviously to a girl across the pool. "We're trying to get you laid."

I hate this word, hate that I've turned so quickly into the kind of guy Rich thinks he can help. But looking over, I have to admit she's a glowing girl, with copper hair and a silver dress that catches and reflects the lights glinting off the water. It rises to the level of the black stone patio, creating the illusion I could walk across and talk to her.

"She didn't follow the dress code," I say.

"Neither did you," Rich says. "That's good. That's your intro: 'Looks like neither of us followed the dress code.'"

We were supposed to dress in country-western or hip-hop gear, depending on which side we secretly rooted for during the trial. For tonight's wrap party only, we're free to vent our biases through Stetsons or Kangols, bolo ties or chains. If only the timing were better.

It's been twenty-four hours since I picked up Harper from LAX. She was back from three months of working for an underdog gubernatorial candidate in a part of Virginia too conservative to believe in dinosaurs. We were driving up La Cienega and I was babbling about what we would wear here tonight: She could borrow my Del the Funky Homosapien shirt, or we could scour Melrose for pleather cowboy boots.

Waiting at the light by the Beverly Center it occurred to me that she hadn't said anything for a long time. It's scarily quiet in a Prius when no one's talking.

She spilled everything at our apartment. She wasn't coming to the party. She wasn't coming to dinner at the best vegan restaurant in Los Angeles. She hadn't stayed the extra days in Virginia just to file hate-crime complaints. She had needed time to think.

She pressed into me and her body felt warm, like she'd been hiking. I was wearing the suit jacket I pull out only for weddings, a clue she hadn't picked up on when I met her at the airport. She pressed harder into me and we both felt the pressure of the small box in my jacket. I had to pull it out then, had to show her the ring inside to see how deep we were and whether the ring could pull us out.

She cried, not in the good way.

"It's okay," I said. "It's not, like, a conflict. You don't have to worry about—"

She looked at me like you look at a dog that keeps barking at himself because he doesn't understand mirrors. "I'll give it back. But you don't have to—isn't there some sort of—middle ground?"

She squeezed me hard and her hair tickled my chin. It smelled fresh, minty. I thought about how I would wake up sometimes with her hair in my mouth. She didn't want to wake up with me anymore.

"No," I said. "This doesn't work for me. And I don't think you should touch me anymore. I think it would hurt too much when you stopped."

Two friends from her department showed up to take her to their place on Kings Road. She had planned that far ahead. Almost everything she needed was already packed in the suitcases she'd taken to Virginia. All she needed from our apartment were her garter belts and Batman comics.

She really was the perfect girl.

Rich jerks me back again from the water, wrinkling the shoulder of the suit jacket. It was on the floor when he showed up at my apartment an hour ago. He said I had to come to the party unless I had a better excuse than Harper dumping me.

"Look alive," he says. "Harpie's probably trolling for dudes as we speak. You want her to get some ass before you do?"

He sounds like he believes himself, which makes him less convincing. Even at forty-five, probably a fake age, he has sixteen years on my twenty-nine, compounded by a VH1 paunch, a presidential-debate tan, and a comb-over so tenuous our network is contractually barred from shooting it at certain angles. His carrot hair is flashier than my brown, sure, and at 6'2" he has a slight height advantage. But I'm in better shape from working out five days a week because I was a fat kid and never want to go back.

He flashes a line of fake gold teeth that, combined with his denim overalls, makes it impossible to say if he's supposed to be a rapper or farmer. It's ridiculous that women would go for him over me but they do.

"C'mon, young hustla," he says, looking back to the girl and slipping into the unfortunate "rap voice" he developed at the trial. "Hit that shit."

On-air staffers like Rich get what they want because they're the ones everyone recognizes. People see his broadcasts on celebrity miscarriages or America's deadliest furniture and invite him into their homes to talk about their son the teenage pornographer or daughter the racist astronaut or husband the snake-handler to the stars. My job as his field producer is to do his pre-air interviews and write his scripts and clean up his messes.

Except tonight the mess is me.

"I dunno," I say. "I think I'm gonna go."

Rich shakes his head.

"If nothing else," he says, "you have to stay and make some apologies."

"For what?"

"The meeting?"

I forgot. We were supposed to meet today with a producer the network just hired from the Evil Empire, our network's nickname for the faceless media conglomerate slightly larger than the one that owns us. "Who was there?" I say, turning away from the pool. I'm afraid he's going to say Philip Wineglass, our host for tonight and the network's vice president for news. I can't believe he would care enough to get involved in one of our stories but that's the kind of luck I'm having lately.

"Come on," Rich says. "Let's get you a drink."

He leads me toward the bar and I look toward the edge of Wineglass's property to his floodlit menagerie of stone animals. Giraffes and great apes and hippopotami gaze mute over Wineglass's topiary huts and hissing Jacuzzis and the smog-dappled canyon below. I trade thumbs-ups with co-workers whose names I don't know and count the rappers and cowboys. Almost everyone here is white, but the rappers outnumber the cowboys three-to-one, a ratio attributable either to white guilt or a retroactive attempt at balanced coverage.

The black DJ mocks us overtly, playing nothing except shit-kicking country and white rap. When he cues up Vanilla Ice everyone laughs that he must not know what he's doing but of course he does.

Rich checks his BlackBerry and tells me one of the Evil Empire's gossip bloggers has already conjured up the usual how-dare-they-laugh outrage for a posting about the party. He holds it up to show me the headline, "MEDIA SICKOS KRUMP ON RAPPER'S GRAVE."

Both of us tilt our heads in admiration. It's payback for our own report on the Evil Empire's wrap party at Disneyland.

We get to one of the bars, a bamboo hut on the far side of the pool. Rich whispers something in Spanish to the bartender, who laughs and cedes his place under the thatched roof so Rich can fill a martini glass with Kahlua, Campari, Fassbind, and something blue. He lights the concoction on fire and slides it down the bar to me.

Drinking is one of the things you're supposed to avoid after a breakup, along with Elliott Smith songs. I tell myself I'm doing it only because Rich drinks vicariously through me. He's no longer allowed to touch alcohol as a condition of employment.

"Chug," he says. "Your girl's watching."

I blow it out and swallow. The effect is simultaneous mouth burn and brain freeze and then everything goes dark. I feel like a computer with the cord kicked out and drink two more as fast as Rich can make them but can't recapture the non-feeling.

I close my eyes and when I open them the DJ has switched from Lee Greenwood to Eminem and the girl in the silver dress is standing in front of me. Her eyes are green with specks of yellow the color of fireflies in Pennsylvania.

"So you're Scott Thomas," she says. "Scott Thomas who missed my meeting."

If it was her meeting, she has to be the new producer from the Evil Empire, which would mean Rich was trying to get me to hit on a coworker. I remember the number of harassment complaints he's settled and feel naïve for not understanding sooner. Eminem implores me to chase my dreams and everyone stops whatever conversation they're having to rap along at the part where he says, "Oh, there goes gravity" and I lean into the bar so I don't fall.

"If I'd known it was your meeting, maybe I would've gone." I'm pretty sure I don't even slur as I say it.

"Keegan Campbell," she says. "I'm supposed to be your hand-holder."

The fireflies are blazing.

"Hand-holder? I think I should consult with Rich's legal team before I answer."

She sets her champagne flute on a hunk of stone jutting up from the patio. When she looks back at me the fireflies have submerged.

"He didn't tell you why we need to talk?"

I try to look innocent. Behind her Rich winks at me with a combined thumbs-up/blow-job gesture I avenge by not pointing out the *Washington Post* reporter slinking up behind him. The five minutes he spent with her in a courthouse men's room have earned him another six months of Catholic counseling with his latest fiancée.

"It's too bad," Keegan says. "I'm working on something you might like, but Ann says your girlfriend won't want to spare you so soon after the trial."

Ann is the West Coast bureau chief, but she's almost never on the West Coast. I'm in her good graces lately because of an explanatory piece I wrote during jury deliberations about the history of sizzurp.

"Great news," I say. "I don't exactly have a girlfriend anymore."

Keegan says, "Oh" and looks down, scanning her thoughts like there might be some standard workplace response. "Suckytown," she finally says. Under all the glimmer she can't be more than twenty-six.

"You know how it is. You have a fight with your—"

"Sure," she says, cutting me off before I can raise the boyfriend trial balloon. I try to form an expression that means "touché" as I lean harder into the bar.

"Are you okay?" she says. "You look kind of—"

Bamboo cracks under my elbows and flaming drinks hit the floor. Keegan reaches out to keep me from falling with them and the bartender says something in Spanish I think means "asshole" as he stomps burning puddles. I offer to help but he waves me off.

"No need, *amigo. Gracias.*"

I look back in Keegan's eyes.

"You aren't driving," she says. "Are you?"

I realize she's touching my arm and try to flex. I can't tell if she lets go then or just before.

"I was gonna get a ride with Rich, but I'm thinking I'll walk."

She shakes her head. "Uh-uh. You'll get hit by a car."

I try to form a look that says "cab?" but it's too complicated. I should practice in front of a mirror when I'm sober.

Keegan pulls her keys from her purse. "I'll drive you," she says. "I'm leaving anyway."

The fireflies are burning bright. "Deal," I say. "Meet you out front."

I walk around the edge of the crowd and drink a margarita someone has left by the pool. Then I speed-dial Harper. When she picks up it sounds like she's at a bar and I'm glad I'm out, too.

"Hey," she says. "What's up?"

"Looks like neither of us followed the dress code."

"What?"

"Let me ask something."

She laughs and my stomach sinks. I need a few seconds to realize she's laughing at someone else, one of her friends in the background. I'm already intruding.

"Hello?" I say.

"This isn't the best time," she says. I know she's drunk because her southern accent is coming out. *Tahm.*

"Last night we didn't really get into why."

"Scott—"

"Is it about the election?"

Before she left I told her I would rather backwater Virginians have the terrible governor they deserve than that she and I go weeks without sex. She acted like that was a bad thing.

"Scott," she says, "you're just . . . cynical."

I try to laugh but it comes out as a snort. "Not as much as I should be. I didn't expect this."

A pause.

"Scott. I just can't be with someone so . . . hopeless."

I affect another laugh, better this time. "Hopeless *how?*"

She says she has to go. I hang up before she can, trying to notch some minor win, and start walking back toward the house. A herd of *Splash* reporters Crip-walk across the path and I turn toward the pool and push past a woman in a rhinestone pantsuit just in time to puke into the water.

I wipe my mouth on my sleeve and weave toward the stone animals. When I get to them Wineglass is sitting on a panda statue with the "MEDIA SICKOS" writer on his lap. He stops biting her neck when he sees me.

"Um, hey," he says, sliding off the panda and helping the writer down after him. "I want you to meet . . . Rich's guy."

He's wearing a one-piece warm-up suit made from some kind of reflecting material. I realize he doesn't know either of our names.

"Yeah," I say. "Rich's guy."

The columnist smiles. Her sparkling grill spells out her name, Candy, and Wineglass sees it and looks relieved.

"*Candy* and I were just discussing the inaccuracies in her latest posting," he says.

"Look," I say. "This is a great house, okay, and I know your statue garden is your private sanctuary or whatever, but—yeah. Can I borrow it? Just for now."

They look at each other and Candy digs a BlackBerry from her purse, ready to type. I look at her, confused.

"I've agreed to run something about how nice the party turned out to be," she says, "in exchange for a night of unfettered access to Mr. Wineglass' life." She smiles at him again. "Beginning now."

Wineglass grins at me, apparently expecting some compliment on his negotiating skills. I don't say anything. He looks at Candy's Black-Berry, then back at me.

"My home is your home," he says. "Go wild."

Candy lowers her BlackBerry. No mean boss story here. I tell her the next thing I say is off the record, then turn to Wineglass.

"Also, I threw up in your pool."

He grips the zipper at his chest tentatively. "Right," he says. "No comment."

They walk back to the party through the legs of a rhino and I reach into my jacket to take out the box with the ring. Even after two months of reading up on color and clarity and carats I'm surprised by its weight, the way you're struck by the weight of a fly you swat with your hand. Before I can convince myself not to, I throw the diamond into the air, trying to imagine its arc into the canyon after I lose sight of it in the softening stars.

NEW YORK, Nov. 13 "We have to talk about Food Pig."

This is how Ann opens the meeting I flew hungover across the country to attend. I woke up alone the morning after the party and realized with fear and desperation I was lying under a hotel comforter. I threw it to the floor, remembering every blacklight investigation I'd ever seen on my network and all the others. I took a shower and found Keegan's business card taped to the bathroom mirror with this written on the back: "Meeting in NY re handholding."

She was dodgy on the phone about why I had stayed in her room. It took several awkward seconds for me to realize she was being vague to spare my pride, not hers. She let me sleep in her bed, with her on top of the comforter and me trapped underneath, the two of us separated by its slew of pathogens. She said I'd told her I couldn't sleep at my apartment because I'd shot out the lights.

She wanted me for the project we started to talk about at the party, but said I could get the details only at a meeting in New York, where people at the network go to talk about anything important. I was annoyed she was so secretive—secrets are a sign of network power, and why should she have more than me?—but I got on the plane anyway. I didn't want to stay in my apartment without Harper.

At our headquarters in Times Square I find Rich and Keegan waiting outside the corner conference room we call the black box. It's called that because the glass walls that separate it from the newsroom tint to solid black during meetings. Before it was the black box the room had blinds but someone kept peeking through and giving the Evil Empire rundowns of our meetings. A hypothesis about lip reading and an eventual sting operation led to a deaf intern's dismissal.

Rich is dressed as subtly as a mobster in his favorite on-air suit and Keegan wears a chocolate-colored skirt and white shirt open to the third button and peanut-butter boots over toned calves that suggest years of high school soccer. She might look even better than she did in a dress. I feel stupid in my dirty jeans and sweater.

In the box, not yet black, a bear of a guy in a double-breasted suit sits at the end of the table next to Ann. She's almost as underdressed as I am, but slumming is her stylistic trademark. Her mother's family is one of the richest in Belgium and trying to look plain is a sartorial challenge.

To add to the drama of the words "Food Pig" she presses the button that makes the glass walls go black at the moment she says them. Everyone looks to me for a reaction, and to satisfy them I form a clench-jawed expression intended to convey simultaneous stoicism and alarm.

Snowflakes kamikaze gently against the black box's lone window and I pretend to be distracted by their beauty or fragility or whatever to give someone else time to talk but no one does.

"Let's do it," I finally say. "Let's talk about Food Pig."

Ann introduces the bear in a suit, a network attorney named Hanlon. I finally recognize him as one of the corporate second-guessers the network would occasionally saddle us with during the trial. He was the one who explained that "gangster" could be libelous but "gangsta" was fine. His neck is gelatinous but good tailoring gives him the illusion of a barrel chest. He leans into the desk to begin a recitation of the Food Pig story that proves to be as long as it is unnecessary. We all know it already.

In 1999, a Green Bay, Wisconsin-based supermarket chain called Food Pig won a $9.4 million judgment against News 10, a local station known for its popular "We've Got Your Back" consumer segments. For one of these reports, planned for fall sweeps, the station sent reporters to work undercover in the deli of a local Food Pig to find out if the store's meat was really as juicy and tender as asserted in a series of recent newspaper advertisements. The story was halted mid-investigation because a customer recognized the lead reporter from a previous undercover piece on unsanitary carnival rides. Food Pig sued the reporter and the station for fraud, arguing they had lied about the reporter's previous service-industry experience—which was non-existent. The reporter was personally ordered to pay back the $4,829 he received in wages for the three months he worked as a full-time Food Pig employee, and he and the station were hit with millions in punitive damages.

"Though the judgment was eventually reduced to $5.2 million, it sent a chill through newsrooms across the country," Hanlon explains. "Since the decision, there has been a precipitous decline in undercover investigations into meat quality. And undercover investigations in general."

Everyone looks at me again. You don't raise the specter of Food Pig unless you're planning to send someone undercover.

Someone like me.

"So wait," I say. "We're investigating food?"

Rich looks at me, his face grave. "Not food. Mexican food."

Ann sighs. She loves Rich the way teachers secretly love the stoner kids, but professional ambition keeps her from getting too close. "We're not just investigating food, Scott," she says. "We're investigating people."

I'm afraid Rich is going to add "Mexican people," but he lets her continue.

"Food Pig was small-time," Ann says. "They had some tough meat. Big deal." She knows I don't eat red meat, just like she doesn't.

"Rich has a source who can document numerous workplace violations," she says, "by a company we believe is far worse than Food Pig. We're talking mandatory overtime, sexual harassment, spying on employees."

"It's even worse," Rich says, "than working here."

Ann glares at him and he flashes her a mouthful of veneers. "Kidding," he says.

I wait a second to make sure he's done, then look at Ann. "Don't most companies do those things?"

She looks at me with the dew-eyed look she gets when she thinks a story is going to uplift the afflicted or afflict the uplifted, ideally by costing other rich, white people their jobs. "Yes," she says, "lots of them do. But not all of them are owned by Glen Ferndekamp."

I nod, pretending to know who that is. Of course Ann sees through me.

"Glen Ferndekamp," she says, "is the president's next nominee for secretary of labor."

Things are getting good. The previous secretary was booted for saying on *Meet the Press* that welfare recipients had to stop sucking government cock. He told the *Times* he had meant to say teat. A labor secretary who violates the laws he's supposed to enforce is an even better story.

"It isn't that any of the violations would be terribly stunning to viewers," Ann says. "What makes them bad is the hypocrisy. Whether people understand mandatory overtime or not, they have to understand a cabinet member doing the opposite of what he's supposed to do."

I look at her again. "Don't most cabinet secretaries do that?"

"Sure," Ann says. "Once they get into office. But this time we have a chance to get one of these guys before he gets confirmed. Isn't that kind of interesting?"

I have to admit it is. I think about *Fast Food Nation*, one of the books that got Harper and I to try to be vegan, and *Nickel and Dimed*, where a reporter works blue-collar jobs to show what it's like for the working poor. This story is a combination of both. Keegan glances over to make sure I get it and I nod that I do.

"The name of the company," Ann says, "is Gringo's Southwestern Mexican Grille."

I've driven past Gringo's restaurants before, mostly at outlet malls in the desert. I hear their ads sometimes on L.A.'s indie rock nostalgia station. A surfer-sounding guy says Gringo's has more options than "those *other* guys" and a flamenco guitar plays to hint that those other guys are hapless, uncool Mexicans, unlike your friends at Gringo's.

"Okay," I say, looking around the table. "But how is Gringo's different from Food Pig? Can't they still sue us?"

Hanlon shifts in his seat and looks to Ann for permission to handle this one. She nods.

"Scott," Hanlon says sagely, "Food Pig is in Wisconsin. Gringo's is incorporated in Arizona."

I give him the look I usually reserve for people who recline in front of me on airplanes. He leans back.

"Scott," he says, "you know those anti-trial-lawyer measures that California always rejects? Arizona doesn't. Arizona eats them up."

I give him a second chance for knowing I'm from California.

"In this past election," he continues, "Arizona's voters overwhelmingly passed an initiative limiting damages in fraud lawsuits—including the type of fraud claim that Food Pig filed against News 10. This means that in Arizona, at least, we'll be far more free to undertake undercover investigations. Once the law takes effect on the first of January."

I give him a look supposed to convey my apologies for thinking so little of him before and my renewed open-mindedness.

"Ah."

Rich leans back in his chair. "And if we're wrong about all this, you can go undercover investigating prisoner abuses. In prison."

Ann shakes her head with the irritation her job requires as Rich adds, "Kidding."

"We thought you would be perfect," Ann says, turning back to me. "You're bright, young enough to work in fast food, and a nobody."

"So I'll get some airtime out of this?"

Rich and Ann look at each other with what must be nostalgia for their own big breaks.

"The minute you finish your report," Rich says, "the whole country will recognize you."

I wish it was Ann who said it, but at least she doesn't disagree. I have dozens of questions about when I'll start, whether Keegan will be in charge, whether I'll have to eat at Gringo's. Ann answers the Keegan question before I have to ask, laying out who's responsible for what.

Rich will get big-picture information from his source, a general sense of how Gringo's works and what Ferndekamp's policies mean for his employees. Ann will supervise Rich's end of the investigation herself. She usually doesn't get involved in stories this closely, and I assume she doesn't want to risk him messing up anything this important.

My job is to get real-world examples from what Ann calls "the ground." Whatever we get from Rich's source has to be backed up with visual, obvious examples. Everyone in news dreams of getting the image that summarizes a story—the firefighter holding the dead baby, the Vietnamese girl seared by Napalm. I'm supposed to capture some visual shorthand for worker abuse.

Keegan will be in charge of my end of the story, Ann says, and will keep her and Hanlon updated on everything that happens while she and I are out in Arizona. Keegan tucks her hair behind her ear, not looking at me, and I try to contain my guilty, secret glee. Even this soon after Harper, I like the idea of Keegan and I alone in the desert. Even if I don't get to run the story.

"Finally," Ann says. "Hanlon."

I glance over at him, suspiciously. I had assumed we were done with Hanlon. We don't usually have lawyers around throughout stories, just at their beginnings or endings, and only then if we're doing something particularly sensitive. We don't let corporate types get too close.

"Besides giving us legal advice," Ann says, "Hanlon is also going to consult with me on whether the news value of our story is worth the legal risks involved."

He sits up in his seat, suddenly alert, as if she's forgetting something.

"And helping with other risks," he says. "Specifically, I'll help Ann gauge whether the story is worth the human and financial resources we're allocating to it, as we complete each new stage of our reporting."

I'm about to ask what he means by "our" reporting but Ann jumps in before I can.

"Basically," she says, "Hanlon and I will make sure what we're doing is worth the trouble."

I'm surprised she's willing to share the responsibility. Maybe because she's rich herself, Ann always tells us to cover stories the way we want to without worrying what corporate thinks. You can't report straight news if you're worried about your company's stock. Of course we all recognize that in the last few years we've given more and more play to drunk actors and dead starlets. We rationalize covering trivial things by saying people's interest in them must reflect some cultural zeitgeist. And if nothing else, the dumb stories earn us the right to cover the important ones.

At least that's what I say. It's what I used to tell Harper.

Hanlon's legal knowledge gives him an excuse to be here, but it makes me nervous to hear him talk about himself like a reporter. I can't imagine Ann accepting a chaperone unless it was the only way to get money from the people upstairs for our hard news homecoming.

"So where do I go undercover?" I ask. "Their accounting office? Human resources? Legal? I used to want to go to law school . . . "

Keegan looks at me, then at the dark glass behind me, saying nothing. Hanlon fumbles with a cufflink. Ann's the one who finally answers.

"Scott," she says, "I think they start you off mopping."

LOS ANGELES, Nov. 15 Harper was into not being into diamonds before not being into diamonds was cool. She could explain Sierra Leone without sounding accusatory, could act sisterly and encouraging when she told people they could buy antique or estate diamonds that wouldn't fund atrocities. I wondered sometimes—hoped, really—that one of the reasons she had taken up the issue was to hint about the kind of diamond I should get her.

The one I found was perfect. A one-and-a-half-carat Princess cut, colorless, nearly flawless, ordered online from a Canadian company that offered certificates proving that no one involved in the rock's production was involved in any type of conflict.

The only problem is finding it again.

I park the car by the reservoir and start looking for a path toward Wineglass' house. I could knock on the front door, but that would mean reminding him of my existence, something I'm not eager to do after our run-in at the party. I decide the smarter plan is trespassing.

I edge into the canyon, using a drainage pipe for a foothold, wishing I'd remembered gloves. The grass is wet, glistening from recent rain, and I wonder if today's sunlight will make the diamond easier or harder to spot. I keep trying to picture the rock and keep thinking about Harper instead. It occurs to me, in the too-clear light of day, and the added clarity of regret, that had she wanted to marry me she might not have wanted a ring at all. My getting her one—even of the cruelty-free variety—might have confirmed for her that I was too middle-of-the-road, too scared to ignore tradition.

I met her on one of the first stories I worked with Rich, an idiotic sweeps report on the supposed trend of feminists doing burlesque. When I first saw her she was onstage pulling off fishnets, smiling at me like it was a joke no one else got.

I found her outside a few minutes later, smoking, and asked if I could interview her. She said no thanks. A security guy walked a dancer to her car and I turned back to Harper and asked for a cigarette. We smoked.

"What's your angle?" she said.

I made sure not to inhale. I didn't want to lose points by coughing. She was wearing heels with bows and a short raincoat and had wide eyes and a small nose. Her hair was tied up but it was too short to stay so it kept falling over her eyes, which changed from caramel to violet and back with the flashes of the club's sign.

"Angle?"

She stood in the flashing lights, considering whether this was worth continuing.

"If you're a human being," she said, "you're probably going into your story with certain expectations and biases. Am I right?"

I looked at the cigarette in my hands, noticed she was holding hers between two fingers and that I was using a finger and thumb. I worried it looked fey and tried to change position without her noticing.

"Well, sure," I said. "But I can't tell you what they are."

She chain-lit cigarette number two, snuffed out number one on the sidewalk. I kept pretending to look at the ground so I could check out her legs. I liked her knees and her ankles and the length of her calves. I liked everything.

"And why not?" she said.

"Because so much relies on appearances," I said. "You know that better than anyone, right?"

She gave a half-bow. "Because I'm a—burlesque artist," she said, putting finger quotes around "burlesque artist" so I would know she knew it was a corny thing to say.

"Exactly."

"So because so much relies on appearances, you can't appear to have any preconceptions or biases, even though you do."

I laughed, for real.

"I can't go into stories having people think I already know what I'm gonna report, or else why would anyone talk to me?"

She didn't look convinced. Something in her eyes seemed to accuse me of fraud. I liked it.

"Okay," I said. "You know Bruce Wayne?"

She inhaled. "He comes in sometimes. Generous tipper."

"Right," I said. "I'm sure he would be." I smile so she knows it's a compliment, then press on. "Bruce Wayne is a cover. The real Bruce Wayne, the person he really is, is Batman. But he can't be Batman all the time because it would be too dangerous. Wayne Manor would be under constant attack. So he pretends to be this playboy dilettante, this guy who doesn't care about anything except chasing women and drinking champagne, which is actually ginger ale. And that gives him the freedom to be Batman."

"Who actually has opinions and does things."

"Exactly."

She looked me up and down. "So you're really a thoughtful guy, and the dilettante I'm talking to is your secret identity."

"Exactly. The neutral, open-minded reporter."

"Which enables you to avoid awkward conversations about your actual thoughts. Nice to meet you," she said. "This is my secret identity, too."

She told me she was only stripping for her master's thesis. The reason she didn't want to be interviewed was that she didn't want to give up a whole year of research for some news story. She was in the sociology department at UCLA, studying sexual power dynamics. I told her not to worry, that we were off the record. I held up finger quotes as I said it so she would know I knew it was a corny thing to say.

The argument in her thesis was that a strip club's business model required every customer to secretly hope he could rescue a dancer. What keeps a guy coming back is the idea that eventually he'll win a girl's trust, make her think he's different from these other guys. He has to think she'll let him take her away to a better place, where she'll reward him with constant sex.

I laughed. Men are idiots. Had she seen any dancers get saved?

"No," she said. "That's the thing. The ones who need saving are the customers."

We smoked another cigarette. I asked if she had maybe the slightest accent and she said she was from Virginia, and held up her cigarette as if her home state explained her addiction. I said if I couldn't interview her it wouldn't be a conflict of interest if I bought her a drink. We moved in together two months later.

She turned out to have all kinds of angles, an array of causes that at first seemed dizzying. Animal rights, conflict diamonds, the environment. She rolled her own cigarettes to stick it to cigarette companies. She just couldn't quit.

I reach the bottom of the canyon, right below Wineglass's pseudo-zoo. This is the farthest I could have possibly thrown the ring. I was one of those kids who was being forced to eat bugs while everyone else in the schoolyard was learning to throw a softball. If I can find the ring, I can return it to the Canadian company and recoup the $14,000 I paid for it. I started saving the week Harper moved in.

I crunch over some kind of dry brush and hear a familiar whirr and hiss. I immediately cover my face with my hands. It's the sound of a high-resolution camera, zooming, from wherever it's concealed. Of course Wineglass would have his stretch of canyon under surveillance. I duck and run.

COVINGTON, Ky. Dec. 7 Keegan lights another cigarette because you can smoke in bars here. She doesn't smoke for real, only when she feels like she's getting away with something. She offers me one and I take it.

"You don't say 'having a relationship with' when you mean 'having sex with,'" I say, fumbling with the lighter. "You use as few words as possible and make sure they mean what you want them to mean."

I'm telling her what Rich told me about being on-air when I first started working with him. Her pupils are huge and I can't remember if that means she's totally interested or not at all.

"And don't say 'having sex with' when you can say 'fucking.' Except you can never say 'fucking.'"

The lighter won't stay lit so Keegan reaches across the table to take my cigarette and light it with hers. We're at the back of an empty bar after deciding not to sit near the bartender because he seemed offended by my trying to order mint juleps. As if they were a Kentucky thing and no one with a California ID could legitimately like them.

"The no cursing on television rule—that's because of places like this," I say, waving my whiskey glass around the bar. "I mean, not here specifically, but places like the South. Or the semi-South. It's weird. Cincinnati's north, right? But just barely. So we're south, right?"

She tilts her head as if she can't quite commit to agreeing. We were supposed to have a two-hour layover between New York and L.A. at the

Cincinnati airport, which is, bafflingly, on the Kentucky side of the state line. It started raining so hard we could barely see out the airport windows and then there was an announcement about the runway being too slick and then about it being flooded. We booked hotel rooms.

"Have you read about this supposed southern tradition of using politeness as a means of social control? Like *Civilities and Civil Rights*? School bus on the cover?"

She shakes her head. I take a drag and blow it out without inhaling, something I used to do when Harper smoked, just to show solidarity.

"All that stuff about southern charm is kind of true," I say, "but they also turn it way up to make you feel rude if you ask for something. Like during the sit-ins. They didn't say black people were wrong, they said they were rude. Like they couldn't even begin to consider the question of whether Jim Crow laws were right or wrong until those kids left the lunch counters and stopped being impolite."

Keegan sips her vodka tonic.

"Or like the mint julep. He makes it out like I'm some kind of outside agitator, but maybe he just doesn't have any mint sprigs."

She looks at the bar, then at me. "Right," she says. "Sometimes 'fuck' is exactly the right word. But we can't say it because people get offended by the right word. You have to say the wrong words and hope they get it."

I nod in gratitude: She's actually been listening to me. We've had only a couple of drinks since leaving the hotel but I was worried she was one of those girls who get quiet when they drink. Before we went out we Googled "Covington soul food" because we wanted to take advantage of being somewhere authentic. When we got to the restaurant I couldn't eat much of anything because the menu was all bad carbs and trans fats. After dinner we decided to walk around but the rain started up again so we found a bar.

Keegan takes a long, slow drag like a real smoker. She says she got it from her dad, that he would smoke during Sunday poker games but never during the week. He could pick things up and put them down.

"I'm the same way," she says.

"You're lucky," I say. "If I ever inhaled I'd get hooked for sure."

There's a short, awkward silence and I wonder if I've said something wrong. She leans forward on her elbows.

"So," she says, "you sound kind of not that happy to be a reporter. That you can't say the right words."

I can't decide if it's genuine interest or if her job might include writing my performance reviews. I ask, trying to make the question sound breezy.

"Oh. No way, dude." She shakes her head. "Maybe I'm, like, technically in charge. But neither one of us is senior management or anything. I'm running this story, but who's to say you won't run the next one? No, secrets are totally safe."

I look in her eyes, decide to believe her. "It's not that I don't like being a reporter," I say. "I just don't like all the compromising. You get into reporting because you care about issues, you want to change the world, and then as soon as you cover something, you can't say anything that makes people think you're pro- or anti-anything. Isn't that kind of . . . hard?"

She takes another drag. "I don't know," she says. "I kind of like being non-committed."

I wonder for a second if she's answering the question I tried to ask at the party—the boyfriend question—then consider whether, after Harper, I could go for a smoking-hot fake-smoker with little to no apparent interest in changing the world.

I decide it's worth finding out.

"So you got into news for the expense accounts," I say, taking a half-drag.

"The travel," she says, blowing smoke. "The exotic datelines."

"Seeing your name on TV, and someday, if you're really lucky, getting to go undercover in fast food."

"Meeting different kinds of people," she says.

"And the lack of commitments."

It takes her a second, but she laughs, letting smoke escape, then looks at me like she wants to ask something but isn't sure she should. Finally she tamps out her cigarette and goes for it.

"Your ex-girl was southern, right?" She looks apologetic, almost protective. "Is she having regrets?"

We've hung out only a few times since the Food Pig meeting, mostly in airport bars, but our conversations already have the feel of jousting. She'll ask something seemingly harmless: Where did I go to school? And I'll say UC Santa Barbara. I won't realize I'm trapped until her follow-up question: Was that my first choice?

I'll laugh—a confession—and switch the questions to her. Where did she go? Brown undergrad, Columbia for journalism. Was Brown her first choice? No, she got waitlisted at Yale. But Brown worked out fine.

She has a gift for questions that flatter and force a concession at the same time. Like her Harper question. It implies that Harper made a mistake but presumes Harper broke up with me and not the other way around.

I pretend to be fascinated by the ashtray between us.

"I'd have to talk to her to know," I say. "I've been so busy I haven't called her back."

She laughs. A reward for admitting Harper dumped me.

"You don't miss her? At all?"

I smash my remaining half-cigarette into the ashtray, enjoying the pressure until it folds and snaps. I give Keegan a smirk to say the phrasing isn't up to her standards.

"If we hadn't broken up," I say, "I wouldn't be hanging out in— where are we? Covington?—with you." I get the tone just right, so she can't tell if I'm flirting or annoyed.

"Lucky me," she says, exactly the same way.

We're quiet for a minute and I look around. The pictures on the walls are the kind you plug in, with lit-up streams and lakes and logos of lite beers. Four flat-screen TVs play *Friends*, and there's a pool table but no cues. The biggest draw of the back room is the vending machine behind me where Keegan bought her Marlboros.

"Hey," she says, turning around to look out the front window. "We've got another break in the rain."

She gets up and walks over to the bar with the slightest strategic sashay. My skin tingles but I look down at my drink like I'm not paying attention. If she wants to flirt with the bartender, fine. But I don't want either of them to think I care.

I twist in my seat, zoning out at the ripped felt on the pool table, and when I look through my glass to check on them, pretending to study the ice, I see him writing on a napkin. I think about just walking out, telling her I'm tired and catching a cab, but she comes back, beaming, and slaps the napkin on the table. It's an address, she says, for a real bar.

The new place is called the Junkyard and its ceilings and walls are decorated with husks of burned-out cars and photos depicting the accidents from which they were salvaged. The seats and hoods have been made into front seats and tables and the bartenders are female and know how to make mint juleps. I buy a round and we find a bench made from the backseat of a Corsica. A plaque says it was all that survived the car's implosion.

"So," Keegan says, "mind if we park?"

She passes me her glass and takes off her jacket, then finds her seatbelt and buckles in. I sit next to her and notice that the strap of her stiletto is smashed under her heel. I wonder how long she's been walking like that and think about the craziness of girls.

We clink glasses and toast the semi-South. This is the part of drinking I used to like the most, before Harper, where all you have to do is swallow and smile and make inoffensive conversation while you wait for the alcohol to get into your and the girl's blood so you don't have to worry so much about your words making sense.

"So," she says, "do you think we've been here long enough for a dateline?"

Bringing up work feels like a taunt. The right dateline at the start of a story provides authenticity, gives a story a you-are-there intensity. Do you trust Iraq stories more if they're datelined Washington or Baghdad?

"It's tricky," I say. "Maybe."

I hope she picks up on my irritation. She could at least pretend we're not just here in a marriage of inconvenience. She's already finished her drink and she fishes out a sprig of mint from the ice. She slides it across her lips, still looking into the glass. I don't know if she feels me watching or if she minds.

"I'm pretty strict," she says. "I don't have a problem with doing most of the reporting over the phone and then just meeting your sources on the ground to get video."

She bites the tip of the sprig tentatively.

"But I do think," she says, "we should actually spend a few hours in the places we say we've been."

"Right," I say. "And talk to the people we claim to have talked to, even if we ultimately misquote them."

It takes her a second to realize I'm kidding. She licks a napkin to unstick the sprig from her tongue.

"And you realize," I say, "there's no dateline or story or anything unless something happens."

I take my last swallow and hold the glass out to her, offering the sprigs.

"Well," she says, shaking her head. "Yeah."

The room seems to get darker and I take her glass, ask if she'd like some fresh leaves. On the way to the bar I think of her as a clever koala, ambitious and inscrutable. I come back with the drinks.

"So," she says, "what were you thinking might happen?"

It's a question but also an answer. I sit next to her and hand her the drink, hoping she doesn't notice my hand is shaking. She takes a sip, watching me.

"With the dateline?" I ask.

"The dateline," she says.

It's been so long since I've done this I want to make sure I'm not hearing more than she's saying. I look for the fireflies but it's too dark and I know if I don't talk before she looks away from my eyes a window will close.

"You'd share a Kentucky dateline with me? You don't have any . . .
commitments?"

It's sloppy but it gets to the point. I lean in close and unbuckle her
seatbelt, then let my hand fall on her thigh.

"I don't have a boyfriend," she says.

We kiss, twisting in our seats for better angles. She tastes like bour-
bon and sugar. Our tongues skid across each other like ice cubes at the
bottom of a glass and our teeth clink: Here's to you. I slip my free hand
inside her sweater and we keep kissing for ten perfect minutes until every
light in the bar comes on at once. We cab back to the hotel and when
we get to her room I ask if this is a pity fuck and she says no, it's a pity
have-sex-with.

NEW YORK, Dec. 15 In my dream Keegan and I are side-by-side assembling tacos in a Gringo's kitchen. Faceless people at the registers are gasping orders into their microphones and Keegan knows where every ingredient is but I don't. She's running taco laps around me while I ask if each customer really wants steak or if they might want to try chicken or fish, and Keegan laughs and slides a ring up and down her finger as she works. She fills taco shells with lettuce and beans and a supervisor keeps checking on us. I know the supervisor is Ann even though in the dream she's Mexican, and the kitchen is in the same place in the building where the black box would be if the Gringo's were in the New York office.

I'm digging under the counter for cubed tomatoes when there's a scream from the drive-thru window. Keegan looks at her hand and holds it up to show me the ring is gone. We go to the window and see an old woman cradling a bloody taco, spitting out beans and broken teeth and finally the diamond.

I wake up and roll over and see that Keegan's pulled the comforter over her head even though I've told her about the blacklights. It's been a month since Harper left and whatever we're doing is better than being alone.

PHOENIX, Dec. 24 Three whiskeys on the plane fail to elucidate my goodbye dinner with Keegan, and the endless line at the rental car office gives me time to calculate my blood-alcohol level. I decide that since I already feel hungover I'm probably okay to drive.

It's just after midnight and I'm mad at myself for telling Ann and Hanlon I'd be happy to spend the last week of the year "getting to know Arizona." I agreed only so I wouldn't have to spend the week with my parents. To avoid admitting what a stupid thing I did with the ring I told my mom Harper had accepted it, then changed her mind, but still hadn't returned the ring—a ridiculous and self-serving explanation, but still better than the truth.

I watch the family ahead of me walk off with the familiar rectangular key of a Prius and feel briefly reassured about the state of the world. I hear the counter clerk cheerily tell them they've gotten the last one.

"Hi," I say, putting my wallet on the counter. "I think I may be a problem."

He starts typing, already looking to his screen for an escape.

"Good evening," he says.

"Hi." I wait for him to look at me but he doesn't so I just talk. "I heard that they just got the last Prius? The thing is, I booked my car last week online and was really specific that *I* needed a Prius."

He stops typing and chuckles almost silently at the screen. Maybe I won't be a problem at all. Maybe I'm the only amusing part of his night.

"May I have your reservation number, please?"

I give it to him and he types it in, looking concerned. But not that concerned.

"If I could ask, sir," he says, finally looking me in the eye, "why do you *need* a Prius?"

I turn my head, bounce it slightly up and down. Of course he's right. I don't *need* a Prius.

"Okay," I say. "I hear you. It's more like I want a Prius."

He turns back to the computer. "And is this an issue about the cost of gas?"

I breathe in, try to stop myself from arguing.

"Not really," I say. "It's more a—believe me, I know this is annoying—but it's more a personal ethics thing. You know, about oil propping up countries that hate America and don't let women drive? I know, you don't have to agree. But I did book the car I wanted, so—"

"Of course," he says. "The problem is, it's not in the computer. Did you read on the web site that you're guaranteed a car in the same class as the Prius, though not necessarily a Prius?"

"Is it necessarily a hybrid? Like a Prius?"

"No."

"Then I guess I'm not super-concerned about the class."

He goes back to typing.

"Look, I know it's not you," I say. "It's the web site. I don't blame you. But I do kind of blame your company, you know? And I don't know the hierarchy of your company enough to know how to get this resolved on Christmas Eve."

He nods, like he isn't really listening, then looks up from his screen.

"Good news," he says. "You've been upgraded. To a Tomahawk 450 XL. And to show how much we apologize for the inconvenience, we're also offering you a one-hundred dollar gas voucher, to offset the added fuel cost."

I bite my lip. The Tomahawk is one of the most fuel-inefficient vehicles on the road. I tell myself to just deal, then ignore myself.

"Right," I say. "I appreciate the effort. And I'm sorry, as a person, to be annoying to you, another person. But one of the advantages of talking to a person, as opposed to booking online, which obviously didn't work out, is you can maybe understand how my little quirk isn't about the cost of gas. I didn't want to be a total pain in the ass, so I didn't get into greenhouse gases melting the North Pole, which, again, isn't your fault. But it's all these little attempts, not by you but by companies like yours, to try to simplify everyone into little problems to be mollified with gas vouchers, which are basically candy, that kind of contribute to a world where—"

"Jesus fucking Christ."

I turn to see a guy in a golf shirt and baggy shorts waiting behind me with his wife and two daughters, both younger than five. The whole family looks at me spitefully as the wife presses the girls' heads together to make sure all their ears are covered.

"Just a second," I tell the golf-shirt guy.

"No, you just a second," he says, his sunburned forehead getting redder. "Some of us need to go see our favorite mother-in-law for the holidays and don't want to wait through your holier-than-thou little speech. If you're so superior you can't accept a free Tomahawk, we'll be happy to take it off your hands."

I turn back to the clerk, too tired to carry on two decent arguments at once. I pay with a corporate credit card, earning the subtlest of head shakes from the clerk—all this fuss and it's not even my money?—then drive to the hotel.

I wake up around ten a.m., angry at I don't know what. I run through the possibilities—the rental car? Being alone on Christmas? Oil gluttony?—and settle on the dinner conversation with Keegan.

She was "glad to get some breathing room before the story," she said, since "things have been moving so fast." Especially since "neither of us are ready for anything serious right now." The last month of studying Keegan's seasonally themed undergarments in hotel rooms has been the only good thing about losing Harper, so of course things had to turn awkward.

In the shower I decide the best thing to do is give her space—no more than a text message on Christmas. I'd considered asking her to Vegas for New Year's Eve but now it's out of the question.

Having no one to call leaves me a whole day to explore Phoenix. I leave my room and head for the lobby, where overnight the workers have turned into Victorians, going about their check-ins and check-outs under a massive, white-flocked tree in the center of the lobby that wasn't there when I checked in. The men are in top hats and silly mustaches, the women in frilly dresses and sexless corsets. I ask a girl on crutches if she's supposed to be Tiny Tim and she smiles that someone finally realized.

"We do different Christmas costumes every year," she says. "Last year was It's a Wonderful Life. I was Old Man Potter."

I'm about to ask why she always goes for the crippled character but before I can she unhooks a frosted cookie from the Christmas tree and passes it to me with a formal "Merry Christmas." I say, "Happy holidays" in case she's Jewish and they're just forcing her to say "Merry Christmas" for her job, then walk away slowly so as not to seem like a showoff in the event that she's genuinely crippled. When I'm on the side of the tree she can't see I try to re-hang the cookie—no need to waste food, especially at Christmas—but it slips off the branch and onto the floor, shattering into crumbs. I sneak out the front.

At the valet line I can't find the card last night's valet gave me and have to describe the car to the new guy, who is dressed in a thrown-together ghost costume consisting of snow chains draped over his hotel polo shirt. When he finds the Tomahawk I tip him a five, realizing as I hand it over that it's my last cash and that I'll have to find a bank before I can get my morning Diet Coke. The valet thanks me "very, very much, sir," before I can ask if he has change, so instead I say, "Happy holidays" with so little enthusiasm he looks offended. I climb into the car and adjust the seat the valet has slid too far forward, then try to pull out of the lot, but the exit to the street is blocked by a van.

I see the woman at the wheel in her driver-side mirror. She stares out vacantly over her dashboard, idling an engine that gets even worse mileage than the Tomahawk's. I honk and she sticks her head out the window, looking back at me with more confusion than anger.

She has one of the cookies from the tree in her left hand and makes the universal gesture for "what?" with the right. There's no universal gesture for "you're wasting my time and lots of gas" so instead I answer with a two-handed "you tell me?" gesture but she just shakes her head and turns to face forward. Finally I see why she isn't moving: an old man with a walker, slowly crossing in front of her van. I mouth the word "sorry" to all parties and the old man sputters curses I pretend not to hear. Finally the van moves and I get on the road.

The sky is powder blue and the hint of cold adds to the holiday spirit that seems to permeate the air, forming a barrier between me and the satisfied world. The bad mood I woke up with is worse, because now I feel more isolated than ever, like I've made a bad impression on an entire new city. I know that in today's remake of A Christmas Carol I'd be Scrooge. But one of the reasons Scrooge comes off so badly on TV is that TV shows only what you're doing, not what you're thinking.

It's easy to be nice and Christmasy when you're anesthetized by cookies and gas-guzzling, assured of your basic goodness by your occasional kindness toward old people with walkers. But it's lonelier to think long term.

In one of the adaptations of A Christmas Carol—I can't remember if it's the one with George C. Scott or Mickey Mouse—there's an early scene where Scrooge objects to Cratchit throwing a lump of coal on the fire at the counting house where they work. Of course we're supposed to sympathize with Cratchit, shivering and cold on Christmas Eve. But maybe we should sympathize with Scrooge: every burned lump of coal contributes to nineteenth-century London's hellish air quality and brings some Tiny Tim-aged miner a little closer to black lung disease. Cratchit doesn't care because he's caught up in his own self-made problems, including a dead-end job that barely pays for his oversized family.

Scrooge's own decision not to have kids reduces the grotesque overpopulation that leads to Victorian-era London's gridlock, demand for fuel, and abuse of child labor. Scrooge can afford to burn coal, but instead chooses to live what we might now call an ecologically sustainable lifestyle.

Of course the ghosts ruin everything.

Working in shifts, they subject Scrooge to interrogation techniques ranging from good ghost-bad ghost to sleep deprivation to terroristic threats. Finally broken, he awakens on Christmas Eve and buys a goose—a purchase the old Scrooge would have considered conspicuous consumption—and rushes over to render paternalistic aid to Tiny Tim. Everyone except the goose has a great Christmas as Scrooge learns to abandon his enlightened, pre-ghost views on zero population growth, fossil fuels, and animal rights. Between the commercial breaks viewers receive the stunningly twisted message that consuming is generous and sacrifice selfish.

Would TV studios roll out a new edition of A Christmas Carol every year if the moral was reduce, reuse, recycle? Of course not. They can't even reuse the perfectly serviceable original version of A Christmas Carol.

Downtown begins to form around me, and I look at the Christmas lights over the car lots. A banner shows a woman in a red miniskirt, its white fur trim just skimming her ass as she leans over the hood of a new truck. The deck is so stacked I have to laugh. Environmental activist types can't win without making sacrifice seem sexier than self-indulgence.

Then I see the Batman billboard.

He stands scowling in front of the Batmobile, hawking a new computer system that rescues people who are locked out of their cars. I remember Harper saying once during Batman Begins how ecologically indefensible a car like the Batmobile would be in real-life and then I realize: So what. Batman chooses his battles.

The Batmobile is an environmental nightmare, yes, but not as bad as the ones the Joker tries to propagate with his schemes to poison the water or the air or whatever he's trying to poison in any given week. Saving Gotham requires trade-offs. Batman understands the need to choose his battles, make concessions.

I wonder if Harper understood him at all.

I try to see Phoenix as it must look to people who live here. Parents of young children might be happy to pave over the desert. They imagine the bites they can prevent by displacing snakes and coyotes. A new parking lot is a buffer against wilderness, a new chain restaurant an assurance they live in a real town. They want to know they didn't leave civilization when they moved here.

I'm stuck with these people. I make a New Year's resolution to pretend to understand them. To make friends with my coworkers and get them to share their secrets I need to be more Bruce Wayne than Scrooge.

I drive around the mountains south of downtown and into Tempe. Buildings give way to open sky and the streets become new and smooth. The temperature falls to fifty-five and the seats of the Tomahawk heat up automatically. I could switch to cruise control and fall asleep.

With the GPS it takes only ten minutes to find the Gringo's where I'm supposed to get hired after the new year. We decided to infiltrate this one because Rich's source said it had "outliers and irregularities." I said I didn't want to know what they were because I didn't want to color my expectations. Everyone claimed to admire my fairness.

I park at the gas station across from Gringo's. This is the longest I've been awake without a Diet Coke in months and the station store is closed. I watch the midmorning light reflecting off Gringo's front windows, thinking about my orders from Hanlon not to go in. Looking up and down the street I see a Holiday Inn Express, an apartment complex, and four other fast-food Mexican restaurants, all of which must sell Diet Coke. But I suddenly want a look inside Gringo's.

The fraud law that's supposed to protect me doesn't take effect until the new year, but the warning not to go inside feels like one more unnecessary imposition from the network. I have to attend the pointless trials they tell me to, cover the stories they say to cover. I'm so frustrated at not being allowed to express myself publicly on issues I care about that I harass innocent car rental clerks. My job is making me an asshole and I need to blow off steam. It's Christmas. I cross the street.

The Gringo's pewter-colored window frames stand out from the brown stucco walls. A walkway leads from the parking lot to the front door, and along the path the restaurant's metal sign stands in a circular garden of cacti and pebbles. Lights resembling study lamps crowd its base. The cloying slant of the red letters in "Gringo's" and the over-earnestness of the block letters in "Southwestern Mexican Grille" depress me about the job ahead, but my mood lifts as soon as I open the front door and smell the lime-scented floor wax. The only time I've inhaled anything so pleasantly thought-clearing was when I witnessed an execution at San Quentin. I was convinced the prison pumped in the smell to make the procedure feel antiseptic. If Gringo's is abusing workers, at least it's getting results.

The restaurant's layout is nearly as pleasing as the smell. Directly across from the entrance is a salsa bar beneath a poster with the Gringo's logo: one taco shell folded into another to form the shape of a heart. The seats are to my left, surrounded by a gently curving four-foot-high wall of brushed nickel. To my right is a hallway leading to restrooms. I walk past the hallway to the counter, where I see the only architectural element that could be ominous: a wall menu that prevents any view of the kitchen.

Gringo's has opted to ignore the Chipotle/El Pollo Loco-driven trend toward letting customers watch as their meals are assembled. The most generous explanation is that Gringo's needs the wall space for the menu often advertised as the most comprehensive in fast food. It's about sixteen feet by ten, part of Gringo's campaign to stand out from those other guys. Learning to make so many foods will suck.

No one is at the counter so I take my time reading the menu, one sprawling section at a time. I can still leave without anyone seeing me, but I would feel like I was bending to the network's will. I look to the left of the menu wall and see a sign on a door, next to the drive-thru area. I squint and make out these words:

Remember The 'GRAND' System
    Greet the customer
    Remember to mention side items
    Ask if they want an upgrade or dessert item
    Nod and smile
    Don't forget the 'GRAND' System

I flash back to sixth grade where we had to create acronyms of our names—one girl said I was Stupid, Chubby, Overweight, Total Tubby— and wonder if the GRAND system could be scrapped. Then the door with the sign swings open and a girl walks through it. I feel guilty for checking her out but I can't resist.

She's small, Hispanic, with thin arms and knockoff designer jeans hugging her thighs. Her frown is hard to take seriously because of her doll's nose and big, maple-syrup-colored eyes, and her hair is obviously well-plotted, kind of a mullet bouffant with soft-looking bangs in front and spiky cowlicks on top. She wears the traditional red Gringo's polo shirt with an insignia of the taco-shell heart over her right breast.

She could still be in high school.

"Hi," I say, as casually as possible.

She looks at me suspiciously and glides to the counter like she's wearing figure skates instead of Chuck Taylors. I notice the baby fat in her cheeks for the first time and look away, up at the menu. I need to make as little of an impression as possible. When the story is over I don't want her to remember that she ever saw me here before January 1.

"Happy holidays from Gringo's Mexican Grille," she says, in the monotone of the unconvinced. "May I interest you today in a Peruviano?"

"Uh, no thanks," I say. "What's in a Pollo Bowl?"

I finally look at her. She doesn't look at my face but at the air in front of it.

"Blackened chicken, onion, lettuce, choice of cheese, black or pinto beans, and guacamole in a bowl."

"Is there any way I could get that with double chicken but no cheese or beans?"

"Yeah, if I charge you for extra chicken."

"Fine, whatever."

I don't want to tell her the low-carb logic behind the order because males aren't supposed to care. She looks at the register.

"Okay," she says. "No one's ordered like this before."

She punches a few keys, then cancels the order and starts over. Her jaw clenches and she looks over her shoulder like she might call for help, then reconsiders and looks back at me, frustrated.

"Most people just order off the menu," she says.

She's going to remember me for sure. I'm the guy who loves chicken.

"Hey, I'm sorry." I try to sound carefree and easy—boring. "You're probably trying to get out of here for Christmas Eve. I'll just get that Peruviano and get out of your hair."

I hope this doesn't make it too obvious I looked at her hair.

She frowns again, still not looking me in the eye, and tucks her chin into her chest.

"Actually," she says, "it might be better if you stay."

I nod like this makes complete sense and she gives me a grim expression back, ringing up the Peruviano. I order the Diet Coke in a medium because it seems like the least interesting size. She mouths my order into the mic, almost whispering, and I sit down at the table farthest from the counter, next to the window.

Looking out at the Tomahawk I see traces of her reflection in the glass as she arranges cups and napkins. I take long sips of Diet Coke, watching her, enjoying the way she moves: fast, precise, in the manner of women who know they're too smart for their jobs. Then the door behind the counter swings open and someone big stalks out like he's been locked inside for hours.

I turn around like I'm checking for my order. The big guy is also Hispanic, about forty, wearing a managerial shirt and tie. He straightens the tie as he speaks, pressing it to his middle-aged gut. I turn back to the window to watch.

"Maria. What are you still doing up here?"

"I'm busy, Frank." She freezes at the register.

"Busy with what?" he says. "Too busy for a Christmas bonus?"

In the window I see him point to his crotch. I take out my cell phone and start pushing buttons to look busy. Maria shakes her head and Frank, the manager, leans in close and whispers.

Whatever he says makes her move away and walk to the end of the counter, where she turns toward him with her arms folded. Out of nowhere he slaps the register, his sudden anger pathetic, proof of impulses he can't control. She drops her arms to her sides and stops backing away.

I cough so he knows I'm here. If I call the police or interfere I'll make an impression for sure. We'll have to call off the story before it starts. Frank takes Maria by her shoulders to whisper in her ear again, pointing toward the back of the restaurant. She shrugs but it isn't enough. He looks in her eyes until she nods, her chin moving slowly up and down. He lets go and walks back through the GRAND door, letting it slam behind him. Three minutes later she brings me the Peruviano in a bag.

"We're closing early for Christmas," she says. "Happy holidays."

In the window I watch the reflection of two employees walking out the GRAND door and then out to the parking lot, laughing and singing in Spanish. Maria and the manager will be left here alone.

"Are you . . . sure I can't stay?"

"No," she says. "But thanks."

I look to her for any sign but she just smiles a sad smile. I go out the front door and she locks it behind me. I stand next to the Gringo's sign with my phone in my hand, a final signal that I can get help. She gives me a slow head shake and walks back toward the counter and out of sight.

I cross the street to the gas station and throw away my Peruviano. I've come to the right Gringo's.

BERKELEY, Calif., Dec. 25 My mom closes the door and says that anything we talk about is covered by attorney-client privilege. That means neither of us will ever have to testify about this if it comes to that and won't tell anyone what we've said, especially my dad. His lack of ethical pliancy makes him impossible in these situations.

He's in the kitchen talking to Nestor and Consuela Alonzo, the Guatemalan immigrants my mom's invited over for Christmas. She compensates for living in a big house in the Berkeley Hills by inviting over as many poor and undocumented people as possible, especially on holidays. As my mom and I took the stairs to her office, Nestor made his first attempt at conversation with my dad: "*¿Que es tofurkey?*"

I ask my mom if the Gringo's situation is as bad as I think and she opens her desk to take out a box of fresh pencils.

"Well, yeah."

"It's bad because Gringo's can say I started the investigation before it was legal to do it?"

"Partly," she says, jamming a pencil into the electric sharpener on her desk. "But mostly it's bad because you did the opposite of what the network attorney told you to."

She looks at the tip of the pencil, avoiding my eyes.

"Normally they'd back you up in court, but in this case they can say you weren't acting as one of their employees—"

"Because I went to Gringo's before they told me to."

She jams the pencil back in the sharpener, a lawyerly scold for interrupting. She likes to explain the process behind an answer, but I just like answers. It drives her crazy so she constantly devises new ways of making me wait.

"Exactly," she says.

I woke up at two a.m. and realized I'd been dreaming about Cambodia, a place I've seen only in movies. I couldn't fall back asleep so I checked my cell phone and listened to month-old messages from Keegan. Then I checked for Harper messages and realized they had all expired. In the first weeks after she left I would hear them by accident while trying to retrieve random phone numbers and catch myself crying in airports.

Around four a.m. I decided I needed to talk to a lawyer, but one I wouldn't have to pay for. I call my dad when I have a question about tax deductions, and my mom when I need to get out of a ticket or break a lease. The airline was surprisingly decent about letting me cash in miles on Christmas so I could get here, maybe because I have millions of them. I didn't check out of the hotel so the network wouldn't know I was gone.

My mom re-examines the tip of her pencil, then throws it in the trash. I think, who is this person? When my parents moved from Pennsylvania to California she waited to take the bar exam so she could spend days with me while my dad helped banks merge in San Francisco. We moved from Oakland to the hills, and then my brother was born. When he started school she passed the bar and went to work for the poverty law center in Oakland. My parents started to get soft and old—the kind of old where you can't tell video games apart—but then when I was in junior high my mom got into yoga and veganism and started aging in reverse.

She sharpens another pencil and snaps it in half. I want to ask what was wrong with it but don't want the conversational detour.

"What's the worst-case scenario?"

She folds her hands on the table as if this is the question she's been waiting for.

"The worst case," she says, "is that Gringo's could find out you went into the restaurant before the fraud law took effect. They argue that the investigation began as soon as you walked in the door, and that the old fraud laws still applied at that point. They sue you under the old laws. The network argues that it isn't responsible for what you did, since you were directly violating network orders. Gringo's then sues you as an individual, attempting to have you held personally liable for any damages they suffered as a result of your investigation."

She looks up at me, anticipating an interruption.

"Go on. This is getting good."

"The network refuses to defend you, having already successfully argued that you weren't functioning as one of its employees. So your parents end up representing you in court, which is pathetic and embarrassing for everyone involved."

The problem with legal advice from your mom is that it has a way of turning into mom advice.

"You know," she says, "you could've just come home yesterday."

"Oh, Jesus. I told you, I had to be there. And I'm not going to ask you to be my lawyer or whatever. I'm twenty-nine years old."

She slides all the pencils on her desk into their drawer. As a mom, she feels obligated to be optimistic and encouraging. As a lawyer she's always in triage mode, seizing on small points about the rules of discovery or the proper way to phrase an objection because these points are usually the best she can make, given that her clients are usually the poor, the helpless, the mentally ill. The laws aren't on their side.

"Look," she says, "none of this is going to matter unless the restaurant can show you were there. Maybe they won't remember you. And even if you're on a surveillance tape I'm sure they don't keep it forever."

I should apologize for snapping but instead I give a compensatory smile. She starts to smile back but stops herself. She doesn't want to let me off yet.

"I know the safest thing would be to quit the investigation," I say. "But I can't. The network's spent too much time already. And money."

She nods as if this makes sense to her, but of course it doesn't. My dad is in charge of making money. She's in charge of doing good. It's the deal they made when they had kids.

"Okay," she says. "Then fuck it. Just go for it and chances are they'll never even realize you were there. You know what?"

She looks at me and I shrug. I don't know what.

"I'm like, proud," she says. "You're giving it to the company and one of the worst presidents in history all at once. I'd love to see this Ferndekamp guy sink as his nominee for labor secretary, and if there's anything I can do—"

"Okay, I know. But that's not what we're doing. It's not a propaganda film. We're just going to show the facts and let viewers decide for themselves."

She takes another pencil from the drawer.

"Right," she says. "That always works."

In the kitchen she tells the Alonzos all about tofurkey, which my dad has been unable to explain because his Spanish is even worse than mine. In his defense, he doesn't work for a news network that provides free Berlitz classes to the staffers smart enough to attend. I scraped through three levels, five years ago.

The conversation turns to family and I pick up bits and pieces. My mom says my brother is meeting his girlfriend's parents for the first time and that I used to have a girlfriend but we broke up and she kept the engagement ring I gave her. The Alonzos say something I don't understand and my mom laughs.

"What?" I say.

My mom opens a bottle of wine.

"Mrs. Alonzo was saying, Scott, that Harper sounds like a total whore."

I look at her with my mouth open.

"Sorry," she says. "It sounds better in Spanish."

I'm surprised at how much common ground she finds with her

guests. She avoids mentioning how she met them, which must mean they're her clients. We sit down to eat and it feels like everything might go great.

Until my mom pulls out her brown book.

"I want to read something," my mom says, "from my favorite translation of the *Yoga Sutra*."

I look at my dad, pleading with him to stop her—Don't let her do this now, not with the Alonzos held captive—but his head is bowed as if we're saying real grace. We haven't gone to church since I was in junior high, but we've heard any number of readings from the brown book.

"This is the fifth of the *yamas*, or tenets of yoga," my mom says, then translates for the Alonzos. "It's the concept of *aparigraha*, or non-hoarding."

The Alonzos tilt their heads, trying to understand.

"We should live with as few possessions as possible," my mom says, "so that our possessions don't take away our true happiness. When energy is trapped inside us, it stagnates and dies. Similarly, when we hoard possessions, they stay with us, and we deny them to others in need.'"

She translates again, making a joke in Spanish about Harper and the ring that I don't understand but that everyone else does, including my dad. They laugh and my mom continues.

"The accumulation of possessions gives us no true happiness," my mom reads, "and so we seek happiness in yet more possessions. But this is a false pursuit, as possessions do not bring us happiness. True happiness is found only through the pursuit of knowledge."

I put my hands on the table and bow my head. I have to admit it's a nice idea, except I can't believe she's forcing it on the Alonzos at a time in their lives when they need more possessions, not fewer. What they probably want most of all is real turkey.

My mom finishes translating and closes the book. My dad says, "Namaste" and reaches for the salt. I look at him—you're in on this too?—but he doesn't look back.

The Alonzos ask a question in Spanish and my mom goes into a long explanation. I gather they asked what the word "namaste" means. My mom's answer seems to be that all people are equal, or that all people have the equal light of God, or share the light equally, or something. The Alonzos look at each other, and I'm sure they're trying to think of a polite way to excuse themselves.

Instead they say at the same time, "Namaste."

TEMPE, Ariz. Jan. 2 Two minutes after the new year began in Arizona, as I was jerking off in my hotel room to a telenovela, a handwriting expert in the network's Washington office downloaded a job application from GringosSouthwesternMexicanGrille.com and began the task of filling it out in the most endearing penmanship money can buy. Ann and Hanlon had spent months deciding exactly how the expert, writing on my behalf, should answer each question, and he quickly went to work. The completed application arrived this morning by FedEx and looking at it now even I would hire me.

Have I ever been convicted of a felony? the application asks. NO, the handwriting says, with a slyly slanted N and fat confident O that suggest amusement at the concept. No, I've never been in legal trouble at all. Not so far. What shifts am I available to work? I was supposed to check boxes to answer, but the handwriting expert ignored them, instead writing "ANY." Each letter slants to the right in a way that implies eagerness and humility.

"Nice," Keegan says, reading over my shoulder. "I need this guy filling out my expense reports."

It's eleven a.m. and we're crouched in the back of an unmarked van from the network's Phoenix affiliate. The monitors built into the walls and ceilings are empty and blue, providing a calming counterpoint to the vibration of the engine. The local cameraman assigned to drive us here has left the engine running out of some overdeveloped sense of drama, as if anything might happen today that could demand we speed off immediately. I can't remember the last time I was in a news van, even one parked for hours, that didn't have its engine running. People like to think of themselves as "ready for action" rather than "sitting around."

The rattling of the van and the smell of wasted diesel make me more anxious but I don't press it because the cameraman and I have been on non-speaking terms since he heard me tell Keegan that Phoenix is "surprisingly non-shitty." It turns out he's a native. I tried to make up for things by adding, "It's even nicer than California!" but he pretended not to hear me.

When I met Keegan at the airport last night there was some low-grade kissing but nothing else. We picked up the FedEx envelope from the front desk and met the camera guy, whom Ann required us to use just in case we needed someone who "knew the local terrain." The cameraman said he knew a perfect spot near Gringo's and drove us here, a block from the restaurant, so we could set up the surveillance equipment Keegan brought from New York.

I had expected miniature cameras to hide behind napkin dispensers and bugs to stick under counters. But Ann and Hanlon said we couldn't risk anything being found. They decided every piece of equipment had to be something I would wear.

It takes half an hour for us to figure out all the wires and tape them under my shirt. The cameraman glances back in the rear view and says how lucky we are that I have so little chest hair. He winks, not at me, and Keegan laughs. Finally she tells me to hold still and slips a pair of non-prescription glasses onto my face.

"Smile," she says, and doesn't. She just looks me over for a long time.

"You," she finally says, "look like a child molester."

I look in the mirror. She's right. I'm a bad haircut and double chin away from being one of those fifty-somethings who are good with knots and dump the bodies in the river and still wear Navy-issued Coke bottles. But the glasses are only part of the problem.

The camera is hidden in the bridge of the glasses, and compact wires carry the signal through the black plastic frames to the left earpiece. The wires exit the earpiece and enter a spongy, neon-orange strap that hugs the ends of the earpieces on each side. Under the cover of the low-hanging strap, the type worn by white-nosed lifeguards in movies with names like *Beaver Patrol*, the wires enter my shirt. Held down by black tape, the wires wrap around to my chest, where they meet another set of wires, this set attached to a microphone taped to my chest. Bound together by more tape the two sets of wires run down to my waist where they exit under my shirt and enter a fanny pack worn backward so the pack faces forward. The pack conceals the wires and a flash deck a little bigger than a cigarette case that receives and stores the sounds and images they send.

The apparatus is awkward, sticky. My rush of nerves feels hormonal. I remember in a cold flash my first day of high school, the fat kid walking into an institution of sweat and coercion and sex.

"Is the pack totally necessary?" I say. "Can't we transmit everything by satellite to a receiver in the van?"

"Only if you want a van following you every time you go to work," she says. "Plus we need permission from the federal government to send signals by satellite. They need to make sure our surveillance doesn't interfere with theirs."

She adjusts the glasses on my nose.

"Under the circumstances," she says, "we'd kind of rather they not know what we're doing."

The plan is simple enough: Walk down to Gringo's in my upsetting costume and turn in the application. But the camera on my face complicates things. What if I see Maria? Will she remember me? If she says something Keegan will see the footage and know I've broken the New Year's rule.

The van driver turns on the radio to a classic rock station playing "Freebird." I feel instantly sick and sad. I used to love it but now it's too wrapped in associations. If he's trying to drive me out of his van it's working.

"Okay," Keegan says. "Ready to roll?"

Two hours later, in her hotel room, we connect the flash deck to her laptop and watch my Gringo's footage on her bed. We're drinking screwdrivers made from room-service orange juice and vodka from the honor bar. The picture is digital-pretty, a shaky P.O.V. shot that lends the Gringo's décor a pale green tint. We move closer together to see every detail.

The camera turns slowly toward the counter with the hesitant movement of my head. I glance over to see if Keegan notices but she just stares at the screen, rapt.

This is all going so well.

The screen fills gloriously with the face of someone who isn't Maria. It's a new guy, pasty-faced and slouching, with a perpetual smirk that makes me think of the words "high school dropout."

"This is him," I tell Keegan.

When we send the footage to Ann and Hanlon they won't have time to watch it. These are just the first moments in the hours of images I'll be expected to capture during my time at Gringo's, and they'll watch only the footage that has a chance of appearing on-air. To speed up their decision-making process they'll send my recording to the transcription department, which will quickly produce a misspelled and confusing written record as semi-decipherable as soccer closed-captioning. I imagine what this document will look like as I watch the pasty-faced head fill the screen.

SCOTT: Hi. I just need to eturn in an applicatsion.

The guy forms a slow satisfied smile, like we've been arguing for hours and I've finally agreed with him. Expanded by the screen his teeth look straight and white—a sign of basic privilege—and I'm relieved the victim of my camerawork isn't poor. A name tag with the name GARY bounces in and out of the shot.

GARY: Rigtht on. Managere's not heree, but I can look it owvr.. Nice handfriwting.
SCOTT: !y@hf.

GARY: Goodod move checking the 'all hours'; box whgere it asks what tiumes you'er avbailavle. If you do that yo're pretty mcuch hired.

SCOTT: Oh cooll.

GARY: They can never find anytne to work the mornings, especaily. I'm in cllasses, Maria has a babauy...

Keegan doesn't notice the way the camera jumps. Maria has a baby?

SCOTT: Wellk great!!!, Thanks.

GARY: And sdon't worr aboyt your referewnces, you can put anything. They npretty mcuh necer call themn.

"Now he tells us," Keegan says. She throws her hands up in showy exasperation and lets her right hand land on my thigh. I cover her hand with mine before she thinks to pull it away.

GARY: Mmnmnm. Uh-huh.

SCOTT: Thannks again f or your help. So... ou'll turm itin four me?

I squeeze Keegan's hand. "Okay," I say. "He's about to say it." I edge closer to her on the bed, wondering if she'll let me take her out to celebrate our big day.

GARY: Hell yeag, I'll tuurn it im. Qwe need more Amerricanz wotrking here.

PHOENIX, Jan. 6 It's surprising how hard it is to get hired in fast food.

It didn't occur to any of us that Gringo's might not be interested in me. We've gone all week without a response to my application, and the panicky teleconferences started on the third day. Everyone has a theory about where we went wrong: Maybe racist Gary's endorsement had hurt instead of helped. Maybe he didn't turn in my application at all. Maybe the manager found it too desperate.

Ann called in the handwriting expert. He showed her books of Ns and Os he had considered and rejected, and produced focus-group evaluations to back up every contortion of every letter. He gave her copies of a 1937 study that he called the bible of persuasive handwriting techniques. She read his research and concurred with his decisions.

Hanlon checked in with my former employers, the ones he had first contacted while he and Ann were designing the application. I had listened in the first time he called my old boss at the pet store where I worked in tenth grade. He warned her that people were checking on me—for added intimidative effect he didn't say who—and said she shouldn't say anything she couldn't prove in a court of law. He advised her to avoid giving out my start and end dates—even the years—unless she still had irrefutable written documentation. When she said she was sure it was at least a decade ago he called her estimate an "allegation." He said vagueness was the best way to prevent a lawsuit.

We didn't put dates on the past employment section of my application in the hopes that Gringo's would think all my old jobs were recent. We omitted my four years of college and eight years at the network. Omissions are safer than lies.

Hanlon reported that none of my former employers had gotten any calls about me. He said they sounded relieved.

Ann pulled an intern off an investigation into midwestern cancer clusters so he could instead research "racism in the restaurant world," which was the exact phrase he used in his subsequent Lexis-Nexis search. Everyone assumed Gary had used the term "Americans" to refer to white people, and that there was some possibility he had learned this coded language from his employers.

With nothing to do but wait, Keegan and I spend the week at the hotel, talking to Ann on the phone, answering e-mails, lying by the pool. When we go back to the room I pull Keegan into hour-long showers that are as ecologically indefensible as they are physically irresistible after the long mornings watching her sprawled out, wet, in her white bikini with green tassels.

We drink during the day, at two-hour lunches where Keegan devours things I wouldn't touch. We have long debates about where to eat.

"There's supposed to be this good fondue place in Scottsdale," she says.

"Oh, nice. I don't, it's just, I don't really eat cheese."

"For . . . health reasons or, like, animal reasons?"

"I used to just not eat meat and still eat dairy, but then my, uh, ex-girlfriend pointed out that cows produce milk only when they've had calves, and then they have to do—something with the calves."

"What do they do?"

I think about it. Accusing her of any part in the killing of calves can only lead to fewer showers. I take another approach. "One of the other problems with meat is that the cows take up so much land for grazing. So even if the cows don't get made into meat, they still take up room."

"That's why I eat them," she says. "So they won't take up room."

She smiles. I don't say anything.

"So you'll eat chicken and fish but not cheese?"

"I know," I say. "It seems kind of half-assed. But I figure they have less complex nervous systems than cows do."

"But what if they don't?"

"I don't know. I think—you can only do so much?"

Her eyes narrow and she smiles again. People always talk about eyes being someone's most important feature but your body says more about you than your face. Your body you can do something about. Keegan's is softer than Harper's, curvy and inviting. Touching her feels indulgent.

We talk about everything: our families, our jobs, the people at the network, the Evil Empire. When our wet heads share her pillows she says what long eyelashes I have for a boy and I kiss the new freckles blooming on her back.

Feeling obligated by our paychecks to spend at least part of each day on our laptops, we keep long lists of search terms we've been meaning to Google. Today mine are "biodiesel," "Bloc Party," and "Nellie Bly." Keegan, way ahead of me alphabetically, has "Philosophy apple wash," "The Phoenician," and "phonetic names."

"Hey," she says. "Did you know that scotomas is the plural of scotoma, which means 'blind spot'?"

We take another shower. I start to feel like not-so-bad a guy. A good catch, even. I should be happy. Instead I feel the warm wash of guilt I get every time things seem to be going too well. After dinner we watch an in-room porn movie ironically but not ironically, and when it ends I tell her I'm going over to the new apartment. The network got me a place a mile away from Gringo's so we could put a local address on the application.

I can tell by the way her mouth twists that she doesn't understand, wonders if she did something wrong, maybe when we were making out during the trailer-park scene. But I know she won't ask because that might imply what we're doing is more than casual.

I drive to the apartment and dial Harper from the landline. She sent me an e-mail around New Year's asking that we give each other some space for the sake of "healing, etc." But I have to talk to her. The phone rings twice and I wonder if she still has the "Freebird" ring tone. She sounds sleepy when she picks up and I'm glad there's no one there to keep her awake.

"Hello?"

"Hey. It's Scott."

She groans.

"I'm in Virginia, Scott. It's two in the morning."

Of course I wouldn't have called if I'd known, but it makes sense she would go see her parents around the holidays. I wonder if they heard her phone.

"We're supposed to be getting some space," she says. "What area code is 602?"

"Well, ah, funny story. I'm moving to Phoenix for a little while, and—you'll appreciate this—I'm working in fast food. Not really, but kind of. I'm—"

I remember I'm not supposed to tell anyone what I'm actually doing.

"It's just . . . this new job."

A long silence I interpret as a yawn.

"Scott, I have to be up in like three hours."

"Really? Why?"

"Things."

It occurs to me that I'm on the phone with the real her and not the imaginary Harper I catch myself talking to when I'm alone. I want to keep her on the line as long as I can, and talk in a low voice to contain my nervousness.

"Okay, but—look, I've been thinking about this a lot. I think . . . I'm sorry, I'm sorry to bother you with this. And look, this may be purely a hypothetical, or not matter to you anymore, but—is there something I could have done differently?"

"Scott." A long pause, like she's thinking of a way to say it nicely. "It's too late."

She sounds apologetic, like she wishes there was another way but there isn't. The idea that she would make this work if she could makes everything hurt more.

"Too late how?"

"Jesus Christ. What else could that mean?"

"I mean, too late at night? Or too late overall? Or both?"

"I need to go now, Scott. I need to sleep. I want to talk, at some point, but after things have time to settle and we can look at everything more . . . fairly."

I wait a few seconds before I say anything because I understand I'm supposed to think about what she means.

"I don't get it."

I know I should have e-mailed, that a call at this hour might feel to her like an ambush. But I wanted to hear her voice, to make her laugh and stay on the phone. To keep us talking until our phones felt hot.

"Harper. I wouldn't have called if I knew you were in Virginia. I don't mean to be the stalker ex-boyfriend. I didn't even choose to be the regular ex-boyfriend."

I wait for a laugh, don't get one.

"Hello?"

"Please, Scott. You want to be fair, right? Be fair. We'll talk. At some point. But not now."

A good girlfriend makes you seem good, too, validates your decency for the rest of the world. Lose her and you're weird again: disconnected, desperate, strange. The worst thing is when you're strange to her.

"Good night," she says. "And good luck with your new job."

PHOENIX, Jan. 8 The tip came in after midnight, the hour when crazy people decide to drunk-dial the news. Local affiliates are required to pass on every tip, no matter how insane, to the network's headquarters. There the night crew files them into informal categories like 9/11 Was Fake, I Killed So-and-So, and They're Trying to Steal My Land.

The call that came in last night, from a woman in the Phoenix suburb of Mesa, forced the night crew to start a new file: Glen Ferndekamp's Nanny Problem. Ann and Hanlon and Rich took the call seriously enough to fly here on a Sunday.

A security team Hanlon hired finishes sweeping the hotel's Saguaro Conference Room for bugs and we file in and take seats at a long table. Ann pulls down a white screen over a painting of a red sun setting over a cactus, then presses a button to project a photo of the woman who made the call.

"This is Carlotta Espinoza," Ann says. "She told our affiliate she came to Mesa from Mexico in 1988, and babysat Ferndekamp's kids a few times. Her cousin was the Ferndekamps' housekeeper and got her the jobs. But here's the thing. She worked for him between '95 and '98 and didn't become a citizen until '96. So it looks like, at least on a few occasions, Ferndekamp employed an illegal immigrant."

Rich raises his eyebrows and exhales. Keegan, sitting next to me, nods slowly at the screen. Hanlon fills a notepad with scribble.

I raise my hand. "Am I the only one who doesn't think this is a big deal?"

Everyone looks at me. I glance up at the picture of Carlotta Espinoza and try to imagine her as a threat to anyone. She's standing in a driveway in sneakers and stretch pants, wearing a baggy shirt that fits like a shawl. She's heavyset, in her fifties maybe, and the only thing she seems to have spent any time on is her makeup. She's waving to a guy around my age who's getting into a Jetta with California plates.

"I mean, I'm impressed we were able to get so much detail about her on a weekend. But hasn't the whole thing about hiring an illegal babysitter just been done to death? Who's the last politician who got derailed for hiring an illegal? It's like getting upset about someone doing cocaine."

Hanlon huffs and sits up in his chair to let us all know that he, for one, still thinks it's a big deal when people do cocaine.

"I mean, really, what if she *was* illegal for some of those times?" I lock eyes with Rich, who gives me a look back that says I'm on my own. "It isn't like she was his full-time nanny. Does she even have proof?"

Ann, motionless until now, glances up at me.

"She took a photo with his kids once. With her own camera. With a 1995 date stamp. It seems possible she's been waiting for the chance to pop out and ruin him. She told the affiliate he didn't pay well."

"How did she become a citizen so fast anyway?" Rich says. "I thought you had to marry someone, like with Russian brides or something."

Ann and Keegan look at him.

"Or so I've read," he says.

Hanlon cuts in.

"It's actually kind of clever," he says. "Mrs. Espinoza married a prisoner. Another friend of her cousin's, a U.S. citizen serving a nine-year sentence. For cocaine trafficking."

He looks at me to make sure I heard: Now do I understand how bad cocaine is? I force a defiant yawn.

"She divorced him right after he got out of prison," Hanlon says, looking away from me dismissively. "But not before she got legalized."

Rich and I glance at each other across the table with looks that say, Not bad.

"Okay." I edge my chair closer to the table. "But I have to think the administration's vetted their man Ferndekamp and has some kind of plausible response to whatever this woman says."

Ann presses the button and the screen fills with a shot of Ferndekamp and the president, each holding a golf club. Ferndekamp's hand is on the president's back, and his eyes are lowered as he laughs at one of the commander-in-chief's jokes.

"Scott," Ann says, "we're not saying we want to help this woman tell her story. We're saying we want to help her *not* tell her story."

Keegan gives me a small, sympathetic smile, as if everyone else has understood this all along.

"Right," I say. "Of course."

"The last thing we need is an undercooked allegation weakening our case against Ferndekamp," Ann says. "And of course you realize that what I'm saying is predicated on the idea that eventually you will make a case against Ferndekamp."

She could have said "we" instead of "you" but the "you" sounds like a dig at my failure so far to get hired. Never mind that I didn't write a word of the application.

"And of course," Ann says, "I'm saying all this under the assumption that there's some case against Ferndekamp to be made. If there isn't, there isn't. We can cut our losses and move on to something else."

"If we don't find anything," Hanlon adds, "we aren't going to go on-air with some allegations that are weak or unfair." He looks at me as he says this, as if these are my favorite types of allegations.

I look to Ann.

"We don't want some kind of half-cooked claims diluting the real claims—or rather, the real facts—that we want to report," she says. "But at the same time, we have to consider the possibility that she could go to another network with ethical standards less exacting than ours."

I turn to Rich, expecting him to add, "If such a network exists," but for once he skips the obvious joke.

"It's early in our investigation," Ann says. "If we think our story is going to be tarnished by this Espinoza woman, we can easily bail out now."

Everyone looks down at the table, unwilling to risk their credibility by defending the story on the basis of what we have so far. Ann's right, as usual: it isn't hard to imagine the administration grouping our story with Espinoza's, and cutting-and-pasting together a news release about partisan critics and personal attacks. People who don't see our original story will see it summarized by rival news organizations, who will include it in a paragraph that also summarizes Espinoza's account. Bloggers will help the White House merge our story with Espinoza's, demanding that our network explain what kind of woman becomes a citizen by marrying a con.

"How do we know she won't just start a web site?"

Ann smiles. "Because she wants to make money," she says. "Fifty thousand dollars."

I tilt my head. "But we told her we don't pay for stories."

Ann nods.

"Okay," I say. "Do we ever pay people not to tell their stories?"

Hanlon shifts in his seat and coughs. Ann shakes her head no.

"Then what's to stop her from going to a tabloid?" I say.

Ann looks amused for the first time. "She wants to go somewhere reputable," she says. "Which to her means TV."

We all laugh.

"What we're here today to determine," Hanlon says, "is whether there is enough of a story to be yielded at Gringo's to justify our continuing this investigation. Especially given this new intrusion from Mrs. Espinoza. We're at an early enough point that it might make the most sense to cut bait."

I'm surprised to feel my pulse pick up. Just a few days ago an easy-out from the story would have felt like a gift: I could have walked away without anyone knowing I broke the rule about staying out of Gringo's. But now, when the chance is right in front of me, I don't want it. I like spending every day with Keegan. I don't want to go home. And I want to make sure Maria's safe from Frank. How often do I get a story that could actually help someone? I wish I could just tell them what I saw on Christmas Eve.

"Look," I say. "I realize I've only been in the restaurant, you know, one time, but in that one, single, brief conversation, we already caught a kid saying on tape that the restaurant needs to hire more Americans. That's just one visit."

Ann writes something down. Hanlon sighs heavily, like I'm keeping him awake.

"We can probably guess," I say, "who this guy considers American and where he got this idea. But, right there, if his views in any way represent the restaurant's, or the company's . . . "

I know the racism angle is probably a dead end, but it's all I have to keep them hooked in. In the normal dynamic of our meetings, Ann lays out a problem, Rich makes stupid jokes, and I come up with some kind of reasonable explanation for why we should delay a decision. Ann gives us more time to work out the problem, whatever it is, and we finish the story.

Keegan stays quiet, leaving the routine intact. But Hanlon seems bent on throwing it off.

"Respectfully, Scott, your entire argument is built on hypotheticals and ifs. We have no idea what he meant by Americans. Maybe he meant the company shouldn't hire illegals."

He catches himself immediately, realizes he's handed me a new approach.

"Good point," I say. "If the restaurant is hiring illegals, that would be much worse than hiring one illegal babysitter, because that would be systematic —"

"Please, Scott, you still haven't provided any solid examples of wrongdoing —"

"And —and - we haven't even started investigating," I say. "I'm only arguing that this is worth looking into, not that we go live with the footage of Gary talking about Americans or whatever." I know I sound a little desperate, but hope something I've said will stick.

"What about this?" Hanlon says. "I'm just talking out loud here. But if the purpose of our story is to help workers, why not bring in some census data and analyze it to show some of the verifiable differences in people's lives based on income? I know it's not as sexy as a personality driven story, but it would be mathematic, quantifiable—"

"Numbers," Rich says. "It's a nice idea, and maybe we'll throw in some data for texture. But we need people in our stories. Personalities sell the news. Real people." He explains it casually, respectfully, as if none of this really matters. I think he's oversimplifying, but it's hard to argue with him when he's so agreeable.

Hanlon tries anyway. "But the data is based on people," he says. "They don't invent these numbers from air."

Rich shrugs.

No one picks up Hanlon's side of the argument. He looks at Ann and retreats into his area of expertise. "Does Mrs. Espinoza even have an attorney?"

"I'll check," Ann says. She writes something down.

Keegan fidgets next to me, then leans forward.

"I think we could use more time," she says, looking at Hanlon almost apologetically. "None of us has any idea how long it typically takes to get hired at Gringo's. This could be perfectly normal."

I nudge her knee with mine by way of thanks but she doesn't nudge back so I stop. Ann looks across the table. "This would definitely be an easier decision if Scott had already been hired."

I shift in my seat, back on the defensive. "Rich talked about personalities," I say. "This place is probably full of them. Just look at this Gary kid. We've already got one right there. And we've got Rich's stuff with his anonymous source, which I'm sure is great."

Of course I have no confidence whatsoever in what Rich has, but anything to keep the investigation going.

"An anonymous source and one bad apple," Hanlon huffs, "do not a multimillion-dollar investigation make."

I see my opening and go for it. "Wait . . . is this about money?"

The look on Hanlon's face tells me he knows he's left himself exposed. He wants us to think of him as part of the team, not as a bean counter. "No," he says. "It's about getting the best stories possible for the good of the network—for the good of the world. Journalistic responsibility."

"He's not one bad apple," I say. "Gringo's hired Gary. They have a counter-person, someone who deals regularly with the public, who's totally comfortable telling a stranger he prefers to work in the presence of white people—excuse me, Americans."

The looks on Ann's and Rich's faces tell me I've come at Hanlon too hard. We're all on the same team. I try to flash some deference.

"I mean, of course I don't know. You're an attorney so you would know best. Wouldn't that constitute negligence?"

Hanlon snaps my olive branch like a twig.

"Don't throw around legal terms you don't understand," he says. "We don't need reporters making legal decisions. You're just gathering footage."

"Okay, let's take a step back," Ann cuts in, clearing the floor for Keegan or Rich to step in and save the story. I'm beginning to not care if they do. The less time I have to waste arguing with Hanlon the better.

Keegan leans forward. "Everyone's making good points," she says. We all look at her to go on.

"That's all," she says. "Everyone's making good points."

We nod. In her minimalism she's found something we can all agree with, insignificant an observation as it may be. She'll be everyone's boss one day.

"Well, the main point," Hanlon says, "is ensuring that we don't devote limited resources to a story that's going to be a dead end."

I look at Ann with a confused expression, then around the table.

"I'm sorry," I say. "I can't do this. Why is a lawyer making news decisions?"

Ann leans forward. "Scott—"

My leg vibrates and I hear the chorus of "Fight the Power." I pull the phone from my pocket and see the incoming number is a 602.

"Holy shit," I say. "It's Gringo's."

Hanlon's the first one out of his seat. "Who's got a digital recorder?"

"There's one in Keegan's—" I cut myself off. No one needs to know I know what's in Keegan's room. "Keegan, do you have one?"

She's already out the door. "And a wire!" I call after her. We can suction cup it to the phone.

"Fight the Power" is already at the part about Elvis being straight-up racist, simple and plain, and I say I have to answer before voicemail picks up.

"Hold it by my ear," Hanlon says, hustling to my side of the table. "I can transcribe. I was a court reporter."

It makes more sense now, his being so haughty about being a lawyer.

"Hello," I say. "This is Scott."

"Hello," says the voice on the other side. "This is Frank."

I try to buy Keegan a few seconds. "Frank?"

He breathes into the phone like I'm already too much trouble.

"Frank Acuña," he says. "From Gringo's Southwestern Mexican Grille."

"Oh. Yes."

"You came in about a job. I didn't think you were going to pick up."

"Sorry, yes. I did."

He picks up on my distraction. "Is this a bad time?" Frank says. "Are you . . . busy with something?"

"What? Not at all. I was . . . in the bathroom."

Rich gives me a thumbs-up. Ann nods.

"Look," Frank says. "Your résumé's fine, with all that . . . handwriting. I just don't want to waste either of our time. The last artistic type I interviewed wouldn't take the drug test."

I try to remember when I last smoked pot. It would have been with Harper, so months ago, at least.

"Hello?" he says.

Hanlon moves away and looks at me with a raised eyebrow: If I'm on cocaine this is the time to admit it.

"No problem," I say. "I don't do drugs."

Ann mouths her thanks. I don't know if it's for getting the answer right or for not doing drugs.

"The other thing is politics," Frank says. "I like all people, okay? I don't know or care what race you are. But I just lost a Caucasian gentleman, an overall good employee, who quit to protest some recent changes we made. Just things to speed up service."

"Changes?"

"He said they were anti-American or something. Are you caught up in that?"

I'm glad not to have any idea what he's talking about.

"I don't think so," I say. "I'm not political."

"That's good," he says. "It's better to not be."

Keegan runs though the door with the recorder and wire and Ann mouths no. We don't want to mess things up. Hanlon's cheek is just inches from mine, on the other side of the phone. I can hear him breathing hard from transcribing so quickly.

"Right after the protest resignation," Frank says, "one of my other guys got arrested, so now I need two people."

I mouth this to Ann and Rich, who look at each other hungrily. This Gringo's must be packed with personality. And with two jobs open, I should be in.

"I'm gonna give you a chance," Frank says. "If you want it."

I look to Ann, mouth the words "yes or no?" She nods.

I tell Frank, "I'm in."

TEMPE, Ariz., Jan. 9 I take the bus for added authenticity but make the mistake of spending my last seven quarters on a Diet Coke from the hotel vending machine. That leaves me without the $1.50 fare I need in exact change and I have to go from seat to seat asking if anyone on the half-empty bus can change a twenty.

Whether no one has change or no one has twenty dollars I don't know. I realize as I meet each new brown face that I look like one of those environmentalists who rides only once or twice a month, for bragging rights, who doesn't know the routine. The driver finally tells me I can pay him tomorrow, and I sit next to an African-American woman in an immaculate white pantsuit and sneakers who holds in her lap a pair of work heels and a purse that looks like it was made from a caramel-colored alligator.

The bus pulls up to the corner of River Run Road and Goldwater Grove and I push open the doors and get out. There's not a river or grove in sight, just a closed grocery store and a Circle K that seems restricted to guys in too-tight jeans who don't bother turning off the engines of their F-150s as they walk inside to buy thirty-two-ounce coffees. I walk the two blocks to Gringo's past a construction site, the morning air and wet cement combining to smell like feet.

I get to Gringo's at 5:50 a.m., ten minutes early. I wish I could buy a newspaper at the gas station across the street but being seen reading could raise suspicions. I occupy myself by walking around the building, looking at it from all angles. My glasses record everything and to feel like I'm not just waiting I tell myself I'm taking exteriors.

Frank pulls up at 6:10 in a silver sedan-SUV crossover ("The REAL hybrid" brags a recent billboard campaign) that makes my Tomahawk seem kind of reasonable. He sits in the car doing I don't know what, then swings open the door and kicks both feet out to the ground at the same time. He stands and closes the door, pushing a button on his keys to lock it, then runs his hand down the back of his shirt and inside his pants to make sure he's tucked in. He turns to me and holds out the same hand to introduce himself. It's cold. The real hybrid must have some serious air conditioning.

"You must be Scott," he says. "How long have you been here?"

He's still holding my hand, as if he'll be able to feel the jump in my pulse if I lie. Does he recognize me from Christmas Eve? He rolls back his head so that he's looking down his nose at me even though I'm a good three inches taller. I wish I could shrink. He seems like the kind of guy offended by height.

"Six," I say.

I wonder if the whirr of the flash deck in my fanny pack could possibly be loud enough for him to hear. He lets go of my hand, giving it a hard squeeze before he does, and turns to unlock Gringo's front door without looking at the key. The air slaps us with the smell of lime. I follow him back toward the counter, hoping it won't trigger any memories for him.

"While you were waiting," he says, "you didn't see any other employees?"

His tone is like that of a private detective giving me one last chance to tell the truth before the police arrive.

"I didn't see anyone, actually. But I probably wouldn't recognize other employees if I saw them. Since I've only been here that one time to turn in my application."

It's a challenge. If he remembers me from Christmas Eve he'll have to say so now. But he doesn't. He just sniffs and raises the counter so we can walk back behind the registers, in front of the menu wall.

He identifies equipment as we pass it. It's like a guided tour from a sleepwalker.

"Microphone to the kitchen," he says. "Cash register. Drive-thru. Long story about the drive-thru."

"Wow."

He turns and looks at me, suddenly awake.

"Wow?"

"Wow" is what I say when someone tells me something boring that they think is interesting. I say it a lot when I'm humoring sources, pretending to understand when they explain zoning laws or composting. Frank's the first one who's ever called me on it.

"I mean, 'Oh?'"

His eyes narrow. "Usually people don't find this stuff very 'wow' unless they're high. And you're not high, right?"

"No."

"Cool," he says. "I'm taking your word on the drug thing. Usually if people say they'll take the test I don't need to send them out to the clinic to actually take the test. But if you really believe the drive-thru is 'wow' I might reconsider."

"Right," I say. "I think I'm just taking all this in."

He rolls back his head to look down at me again, then turns and continues the tour. I look for anything Ferndekamp wouldn't want a reporter to notice.

Frank flips a switch and the overhead lights flash on in sections, cycling from the windows to the wall. Then he leads me to the back of the restaurant, flipping more switches. I glance at the GRAND sign, pretending it's new to me.

Frank opens the door he came out of on Christmas Eve to lead me back. It opens to a long hallway, with a cutout entrance to the kitchen on the immediate right. This seems like the most likely place for things to go badly. I imagine stretched-out hunks of meat or entire chickens burning on the grill, which runs the length of a wall. Empty tables in the middle of the room make me think of cutting, hacking. The surfaces are metal and I wonder if that's because wood holds blood.

Frank walks us past the kitchen to the end of the hall and unlocks another door, opening and then partially closing it behind him. I hear him turn on a TV as I look at the bulletin board outside his office, scanning the signs and announcements: a bilingual, laminated poster from Arizona's Division of Industrial Relations about time off for voting, minimum wage, and the rights of pregnant employees; a fill-in-the blanks list with spaces for police, fire, and ambulance numbers, all blank; and a dry-erase board where someone has written *"puta."* Frank comes out of the office and hands me a balled-up polo shirt. I hold it up and see it's the same kind Maria was wearing, with the taco-shell heart.

"As of last summer, this is the entire Gringo's uniform," he says. "They decided to get rid of hats."

It's too bad they did. If I had a hat we could sew the camera into it and I wouldn't have to wear the child-molester glasses.

"Also, no studded belts, no facial jewelry, and you must wear black sneakers. Not Chuck Taylors, whatever you might see other employees wearing."

I remember Maria was wearing Chucks.

"You can change in the bathroom. Any questions?"

"Just one," I say. "Can I wear my fanny pack with my uniform?"

If not we need to find some new way to hide the flash deck, probably in the region of my crotch. I hope he says yes.

"Why?" He looks at the bundle at my waist and sneers. "What's in the pack?"

Has he caught interlopers this way before? What does he think is in the pack? He raises an eyebrow and I remember he's worried about drugs, not surveillance.

"Well, everything!" I say, as if I'm surprised he's never worn one. "Mostly, you know, lip balm. For the sun?"

He stares at me.

"I mean, it's not so bad now, not to you, but I have really sensitive, uh, lips. They get really dry if I don't use balm, and if I keep it in my pants pocket it can go through the laundry. But not just lip balm. My wallet and . . . "

If he asks to see my lip balm this is over.

"It's not in the rules one way or the other," Frank says. "Sure. Wear the fanny pack. It's not like you'll get much pussy in the uniform anyway."

I laugh, but not for the reason he thinks. I'm imagining a montage of managerial errors—shot after shot of Frank saying things he shouldn't—followed by a cutaway to a labor rights attorney who can soberly provide the definition of a hostile work environment with just the slightest judgmental tone.

"So look," Frank says. "You can ask your real question now."

This confirms it. He has to know about Christmas Eve. As soon as he mentions the first time we saw each other the network will know I was here before I was supposed to be. I wish he had made me take off the fanny pack so this wouldn't be recorded.

"Real question?" I laugh. "I don't have a real question."

His expression switches to impatience. "I see," he says. "So you're planning to work for free."

I feel the red tingling on my forehead and cheeks. In all our weeks of plotting to get me hired, it never occurred to anyone at the network that I might want to know how much I would get paid.

"Sorry," I say.

He just looks at me. He still isn't going to tell me until I ask. It's a game now.

"Sorry," I say again. "How much do you—right. I'm asking how much."

"How much we pay?"

"Right," I say. "How much you pay."

"Six-fifty an hour," he says, his smile adding, Wasn't that easy? I don't know if he's pleased with himself because I had to ask or because he makes so much more than I will. Rich says his source tells him that Gringo's managers make up to $60,000 a year, about two-thirds of what I make at the network.

On my way to the bathroom I try to calculate what my annual salary would be here but get depressed and give up. I signed up to work thirty hours a week so I would have enough time for meetings and travel for my real job, but most Gringo's employees can't get more time than that anyway. Rich's source says the company tries to keep people part-time so they won't qualify for health benefits.

I lock myself in a bathroom stall and carefully remove my shirt to avoid pulling up any of the masking tape holding my wires in place. The bathroom is nothing fancy, but it's still the cleanest I've been in that doesn't have a towel valet offering to dry your hands for tips. Pulling on the new shirt I think about how I hate places with towel guys. What I hate the most is that the only way you can protest someone having a job so demeaning is to refuse to tip them until the bar or restaurant or whatever decides there's no market for their services. And who's punished by that? I look at myself in the mirror in my new shirt and feel for the first time like one of the towel guys, not one of the people too sympathetic to tip them.

When I get back to the rear of the restaurant two more employees have arrived and Frank is chewing them out in the kitchen for being *tarde*, a word my last Berlitz instructor would use to announce my arrival to class. My new colleagues look like easy-listening stars—they're youngish, Hispanic guys with thin mustaches and feathered hair, falling to their shoulders in waves. Frank's Spanish is stilted, uncertain. It occurs to me that the purpose of his monologue may be practice. Finally he mentions *el nuevo Gary* and the employees glance up at me and share a snicker.

I laugh, but too late. The new Gary. The new racist white guy. So this is the kind of boss Frank is. Dividing us on the basis of race and language must be the laziest way to play us off each other.

"Scott," Frank says, "I want you to meet Juan and Carlos, two of our line chefs."

I have to win them over, show them I'm not like Gary, no matter what Frank tells them. Would Gary address them in Spanish?

"*Hola,*" I say. "*¿Como estan?*"

They look at each other.

"Hi," Juan says. "Pleased to meet you."

"Good morning," Carlos adds. "How are you?"

I've lost them. I am the new Gary after all. The rule for addressing Spanish-speaking people in the U.S. is the opposite of the rule for addressing French people in France. In France you start out speaking French so no one thinks you expect them to know English. In the U.S. you start out in English so no one thinks you expect them not to.

Juan and Carlos step forward to shake hands, but I know it's only because the boss is watching.

"I'm trying to get Scott trained," Frank says, "to work the drive-thru."

Huge laughter now from Juan and Carlos. I know I'm supposed to feel insulted but I don't understand why I would be. I've just been promoted to the front, on my first day, while they'll be stuck back here making burritos. Frank leads me out to the hallway.

"You understand anything I was telling Juan and Carlos?"

"Not to be late."

"Not bad. You learn Spanish in a kitchen?"

He must have barely looked at my résumé. None of my old jobs were in restaurants.

"High school," I say, and instantly regret it. My answer leaves me exposed to lots of other questions, like where I went and what I've done in the years since.

"Mm," he says. "I've been taking classes. ASU. They thought I could speak Spanish when they made me manager, and I've had to catch up."

I get it: No one just handed him two languages. He's too proud of his own story to worry about mine.

"If your Spanish is all right," he says, "maybe I can skip you past cleaning and toss you into the kitchen today." He nods as he says it, agreeing with his own plan. He seems proud of how easily he can move us around, how totally he controls us here. I hope this comes across on camera.

In the kitchen, Juan and Carlos seem happy to have me back. I start to wonder if I read too much into their laughter. Maybe they're a couple of joyous guys, satisfied just to be doing their jobs. Maybe I should try to do the same.

Frank gives Juan and Carlos a few instructions I'm not quick enough to understand and disappears down the hall to his office. They pass me items for prepping. Lettuce and tomatoes and pre-grated cheese need to be removed from their plastic bags. Eggs and chicken need thawing. Pull the meat from last night's marinade. Mash the guacamole so the dry, hard part mixes with the rest.

Juan and Carlos explain these duties through hand gestures and English that turns out to be no better than my Spanish. All of us can manage casual greetings, but beyond that all we can say is sorry.

"*Lo siento, mis amigos. Necesito aprender mas español.*"

"No, the error is mine," Juan answers. "I have resolved to improve my English."

Friendly greetings and apologies seem like a good start, and I regain hope that Juan and Carlos and I can be friends. Or at least the kind of acquaintances who volunteer detailed accounts of horrendous labor abuses.

My linguistic shakiness makes me especially eager for clarification of their suggestion that I, the brand-new employee, fire up the fryer, which must be the most dangerous job in the kitchen since none of the others involve intense heat. But they insist with huge smiles that "*si, por supuesto,*" this is the way it should be. They each have their own set of explanatory hand gestures about fryer operation, none of which seem to overlap. As I start turning dials they begin a manic song, the kind mythical dwarfs might sing after vanquishing a bad troll in the kind of movies that make me fall asleep. I make a mental note to have the lyrics translated and transcribed.

Ten minutes before seven, after my trial-and-error flipping of fryer switches results in the device's first stirrings of heat, Frank comes back and spits out the word "motherfucker," first in English, then Spanish. Juan and Carlos point to me accusingly, then raise their palms to demonstrate either that they had nothing to do with me turning on the fryer or that they're unarmed.

No, Carlos explains, of course he didn't tell me to do it. Juan elaborates too quickly for me to pick out any Spanish words except the ones for "liar," "racist," and "drugs."

I announce, "*No uso las drogas*" as I try to remember how to phrase the other necessary denials. I also need to learn to say, *But I thought we were friends.* Frank spins to stare at me, his nostrils flaring.

"So you know the word for drugs," he says.

I start to say it's one of the easy words but he throws up a hand and uses the other to massage his own neck. He motions soundlessly for me to follow him to the front of the restaurant and when we get there I see a mop and pail of sweet-smelling water.

I nod. I've studied my office cleaning lady any number of times over the last few weeks, admiring her speed and meticulousness, preparing for this very moment. I work the corners first, avoiding eye contact with ASU students who come in for breakfast in their flip-flops and pajamas. Handling the counter is another employee, a husky blonde girl named Bethany. Frank spares her the Maria treatment, whether because of the customers or the huskiness I don't know. I mop until noon and take the bus back to the hotel.

At night, the network's transcription service presents us with an English translation of Juan and Carlos' song. The transcription robs the song of its dwarfy meter, but for once it doesn't have a single typo. Keegan and I go to a Scottsdale tequila bar to celebrate my first day at work, and by our fourth $22 shots we've memorized the song in its entirety.

When the white guy leaves
The sour cream is seized
And we fill it with ejaculate
To serve to the assholes
Tomatoes are a fine thing
To place within one's asshole

And then dice and place in nachos
To serve the real assholes
It's a humble job yes
But the benefits are mighty
Like the joy of putting semen
In shredded cheese for assholes
Kiss my ass gringo
Kiss my ass Gringo's
Behold your mild comeuppance

TEMPE, Ariz., Jan. 10 "Yesterday was partly my fault," Frank says. "I shouldn't have let you in the kitchen without telling you about the STAC system."

It's 6:10 a.m. and he was only five minutes late today. He leads me to the booth where I watched his and Maria's reflections, and as we sit I search his face for any sign he's done it on purpose but can't find any. I think it's time to relax.

"The fryer is in the past," he says. "Today let's try something fun."

I'd been hoping to spend the day mopping in corners. The tequilas and twisting all night in Keegan's damp sheets have left me drained and lightheaded. On the bus my stomach felt adrift, paddling under the sun.

Frank passes me a pamphlet that says "STAC: Sanitation, Temperature, Attitude, and Cleanliness." I wonder if anyone's explained the STAC system to Juan or Carlos.

"These are just some basic principles we follow when handling food," Frank says, smoothing his tie. "Give it a read and let me know if you have any questions."

"Actually," I say, "I have one question already."

"Fire away."

Frank looks pleased. I guess most people don't ask questions. I'm sorry I'm about to disappoint him but I can't stop myself.

"How is sanitation different from cleanliness?"

He exhales, expunging his momentary satisfaction.

"It's in the pamphlet," he says.

"I'll read it," I say. "But you see where I'm going with this, right? I know it's not you, but the people who write the pamphlet—why not combine the sanitation and cleanliness sections?"

He nods as if there's a tremendous bureaucracy involved, not just in writing the pamphlet, but in moving his head up and down.

"I think you'll be impressed," he says, "by how well they handle that very issue."

He stands up to leave me alone at the table. I open the pamphlet and flip through each section. The Sanitation section begins with a three-panel cartoon about the importance of handwashing. Then there's a bit about how employees are allowed to eat only in the dining area on designated breaks, and how nibbling in the kitchen is both unsanitary and theft. As if there's any risk of me eating anything here after yesterday. Sanitation is followed by an interesting section about how to check the Temperature of food. The pamphlet says this is done constantly at Gringo's, not just when the Board of Health is investigating a complaint. The next bit is about bringing a good Attitude to all sections of the STAC system. It's the shortest section, and is obviously only there to justify the vowel.

Finally we get to the specifics: how to do everything involved in Cleanliness, from dusting off the top of the refrigerator to mopping the floors. This section, by far the most informative, contains the secret formula for the lime floor wax (one bottle cap of something called "Lim Lam" in a two-gallon bucket of hot water). It takes three minutes to read, more time than the others.

The pamphlet ends with an X through a picture of a cartoon mouse wearing a sombrero and a warning that only by strictly following the STAC system can we prevent unwanted visitors. I find something cruel about Gringo's making the effort to give the mouse anthropomorphic features only to demonize him. If he's smart enough to find a mini-sombrero he's smart enough to master STAC.

Frank appears again at the table.

"Good," he says. "You're done. Any questions?"

"Nope, made a lot of sense."

He smiles. "So you saw the separate sections on sanitation and cleanliness?" He says it like I was misunderstanding something before.

"Yup," I say. "Two separate sections."

He frowns: Here we go again. "Are you agreeing that there are two separate sections, or that there should be two separate sections?"

I clench my jaw like I'm really puzzling it over. "Well, one thing I thought about is that if they moved all the Cleanliness stuff into Sanitation, they'd have to call the whole thing the STA system."

Frank doesn't laugh. "But then it wouldn't be as easy to memorize," he says.

"No."

Frank sits down, presses one hand into the other. "The thing is," he says, "not everyone here is as smart as you. We have to write it for the people who may not have your sophistication or language skills."

It's one of those compliments that I can't agree to without insulting everyone else. I want to make a small point, gently drop hints to him that he should gently drop hints to the Gringo's higher-ups that their training materials don't have to be so condescending. Maybe Juan and Carlos would feel more invested in Gringo's if they were treated with respect. Word games are alienating. Frank looks at me with an expression that says, Are we done? But of course we aren't.

"What I guess I'm just wondering," I say, "is whether they could have just combined Sanitation and Cleanliness at the end and called it the TASC system?"

Frank puts his palms flat on the table.

"We like to put Sanitation first because sanitation comes first here," he says. "If that's okay with you."

I glance in the window, amused to see the reflection of myself in a Gringo's shirt. To anyone outside I would look like a real employee. "You're right," I say. "I think it should come first. I guess I'm just not used to learning from pamphlets."

"Yeah," Frank says. "They used to do videos but no one liked those."

"What about this? What if they combined Sanitation and Cleanliness at the beginning, but just called that section Sanitation, and then, at the end, they said 'Re-read Sanitation section,' and they called the whole thing the STAR system?"

He reaches across the table to take the pamphlet. "Look," he says, "do you want to work here or not?"

I smile, wait for him to smile back to acknowledge what a cheap tactic this is, resorting so quickly to the fact that he's the boss and I'm the employee. But his face is a blank, as if he genuinely doesn't care if I say yes or no.

"Of course I want to work here."

He nods slowly, like it would have been easier if I'd said no.

"The thing is," he says, "I'm gonna need you to do me a favor and read that a couple more times, and then we'll talk again."

This is the first time in years I've had a job where I'm not encouraged to argue. It's like losing part of my brain.

"I think I get it already," I say, but Frank is already getting up. The front door swings open and we both turn to look.

Maria.

I raise the pamphlet to hide my face. If she says anything to trigger Frank's memory of Christmas Eve he can fire me on the spot and use STAC as an excuse. Ann and Hanlon will see the footage from my glasses and make me explain and then I'll probably be fired from my real job, too.

I lower the pamphlet slowly, hoping to scramble her recognition by hiding part of my face. Frank crosses his arms as she walks up to us, stopping a few feet from the table. She ignores Frank and looks down at me, making a clicking noise with her mouth like her gears are turning. I would turn off the camera if only there was a way to reach into the fanny pack without appearing to touch my groin.

"Oh, God," Maria says, turning to Frank. "You're making him learn STAC?"

Frank lowers his arms. "You're late."

"Sorry," she says. "Female problems." She smiles at me like I might relate.

"We need to talk about you being on time," he tells her. "In my office."

She looks at me again, but this time she winks. She remembers. I shift my eyes slowly to Frank's to see if he saw the wink but he's looking at the pamphlet on the table.

"Come on, Frank." Maria rolls her eyes until they land again on mine. "Shouldn't I meet my new *co-worker?*"

She's a different girl than she was the other day. I wonder if my presence—the presence of anyone else—is the source of her confidence. I send desperate mental signals that she should just go with him, that I'm on her side but that for now I need to keep my cover.

Frank slides the pamphlet under my nose.

"Read it again," he says, and walks past Maria toward the counter. He looks back at her, expecting her to follow, but instead she heads toward the front door.

"I'm going to the ladies' room first," she says. "It's an emergency."

Frank mumbles something as he lifts the section of counter to go to the GRAND door. As he closes it behind him Maria spins balletically and walks back to me.

"You look different."

I look down at the pamphlet. My stomach feels like it's taking on cold water. I'm forgetting how to swim.

"Different how?"

She exhales, upwards, inflating her bangs. I'm going to make this hard.

"You know how," she says.

I open the pamphlet. "I'm sorry," I say. "I don't think we've met."

She dips her chin, smiles a smile that seems more amused than surprised: Do I think I'm going to save her? Is that why I'm here?

"Well," she says, "I beg your forgiveness, stranger."

She walks up and holds out her hand mock daintily, like a girl in a silent movie. It feels a dare to kiss it but instead I hold out my hand and we shake.

"I'm Maria," she says. "It's a pleasure to meet you, for the first time."

"Scott."

"Nice to, um, meet you," she says.

I keep my voice as flat and uninterested as possible for the benefit of whoever might hear the recording of our exchange.

"Nice meeting you, too."

The sooner we can get to our next second meeting, the easier things will be. She turns and walks slowly to the back of the restaurant.

"You must've really messed up," she calls from the counter, "if he's making you read that."

TEMPE, Ariz., Jan. 12 In the mail forwarded to me from L.A. is a wedding invitation from Richmond, sent to Harper at my address. Whoever sent it knows Harper well enough to invite her to the ceremony but not well enough to know she's broken up with her boyfriend and moved out, which isn't all that surprising considering that Harper was never all that big on keeping in touch with her Virginia friends.

She went to an all-girls Episcopal school that was apparently where all the most successful people in Richmond sent their kids. Her classmates were always invited to each other's weddings because their fathers could afford it. The unwritten rule was that if you missed three in a row people started rumors you were in detox. The first time I went to Richmond was because Harper had just missed two.

We got there a few days before the wedding so I could meet her parents. Her dad was worried I believed the stereotypes about backward southerners and I was afraid he believed the accuracies about smug West Coasters. We tried to subvert each others' presumed biases. He took us to a tapas place on the first night and asked if I knew Harper was named for Harper Lee.

"Who?"

He looked up from a plate of ceviche. "Southern writer? *To Kill a Mockingbird*?"

"Oh, right." I adjusted my napkin. "One of my all-time favorites."

Harper and her parents raised their glasses in salute and I held up the shoddy beer I'd only ordered to show how down-home I was. Harper told me later I'd scored huge points, that she'd assumed I hadn't read it because it was usually the first thing people mentioned when she told them her name.

It was too late to tell her I hadn't.

Her dad took us for long drives to see lawns and ivy and crayon-red houses that looked secure. I wondered aloud how many had been plantations and Harper's dad explained eagerly that his family's house had been built in the 1980s. I noted with approval that it was normal-sized and not as gaudily extravagant as the ones we had to visit for three days of pre-wedding events that included brunches and cocktail receptions and a ladies' tea and a men's golf outing that I opted out of because come on.

The wedding was black tie. I borrowed her dad's tuxedo and a Jerry Garcia cummerbund he insisted I wear. Harper wore an Oleg Cassini dress her mom had worn to her senior prom and had finally agreed to let Harper have taken in to a size four. The ceremony was at a church and included the Lord's Prayer, which I knew from when my parents took us to a Presbyterian church during their "seeking" phase, before they came to understand the concept of predestination and how un-democratic it is.

The reception was held at a country club where we stood out on a patio overlooking the golf course. Harper's old classmates were now dating or married to investment bankers. Everyone except me smoked and the air was sticky and hot. I mentioned some distant relatives from Tennessee, vying for some kind of southern credibility, but got more discouraged with each new introduction to a Kiplinger or Tately or Tinsley or Byrd. I couldn't keep their names straight, much less make conversation. I drank too much champagne and hid out in a study by the bathrooms that housed hundreds of hilarious books about great Confederate victories. None of the ones I flipped through found room to mention that the North ultimately kicked total ass.

I made Harper come back to the study almost as a test, to see if she shared the local fixation with failure. She listened charitably as I read random passages aloud, not even calling me out when my accent collapsed into riverboat Cajun. Then she said we had to get back to the reception to prevent rumors she had passed out.

The party moved inside and I switched from champagne to scotch, poured by an elderly black man named Edward with whom I made a point of discussing the day's humidity. I hoped that someday, when he looked back on all the drunk white people he had served, he would think of me as one of the good ones. All the guests were white and everyone working was black, including a waiter who had been on the academic decathlon team that Harper said beat her school's every year.

She and I got separated and the bride's maid of honor dragged me into a conversation near the bar about how Virginia compared to California. I mumbled something about how green Virginia was and she announced to the handful of cousins drinking around us that she had been to Disneyland when she was twelve and liked Richmond better.

"The weather's nice out there, I'll give you that," she said, looking at her cousins instead of me. "But I heard in L.A. they have rats in the palm trees, and all them gay guys."

I tried to think of something tactful. No, there were no rats. Yes, there were gay guys. I resolved to be civil because she hadn't said anything overtly intolerant about all those gay guys, only that they existed. Like rats.

"Don't get me wrong," she said, "I love fags. Some of my best friends are fags."

I blinked at her. The word was pejorative, but she was using it to refer to some of her best friends. This was borderline and I could let it go, especially at a wedding.

"And y'all talk about us having blacks," she said, "but y'all have Mexicans."

I tried to smile. "What do you mean by . . . have?"

"Don't get me wrong," she said, waving her hands, pulling up a strap on her dress. "I love Mexicans. I wish we had more. They work way harder than nig—"

I turned and faked a coughing fit, looking up to see if Edward had heard her. He was too busy making martinis. I coughed toward the bathroom like I had something caught in my throat, then hid in the study again to cheer myself up with reminders of how badly these people lost the Civil War.

Harper found me again. "If you can just keep it in check for two more hours," she said, "I'll dress up in my school uniform when we get home and you can have anything you want."

I said I knew she was bluffing. There was no way she would risk it at her parents' house, no matter how cool her dad was. She pushed me backward into a leather armchair and sat on my leg. "Come on," she said. "This place is, like, my home. Can you at least try?"

I frowned, looking for sympathy.

"I know," she said. "Look, I left for a reason. But it's still home."

We walked into the dining room as the toasts were ending. The groom's father, a Tulsa oil executive, was droning on about the rich traditions the newly joined families would now share: "Golf . . . Oklahoma football . . . Indian guides . . . Indian guides . . ."

I had no idea whether "Indian Guides" was the name of some secret society or if each of the families literally had Indian guides, the way Californians "have" Mexicans. We drank more and I dragged Harper outside to make out on the golf course.

When we went back inside a singer (black, technically working) was serenading the bride and groom to Bill Withers' "Just the Two of Us," which despite everything is a gorgeous, perfect song. There were more dances until finally the singer called out, "C'mon, ladies! You know you want to take off them shoes!" and the band (black) swung into "Hey Ya" because there were still people (white) who weren't yet sick of "Hey Ya." We danced with Harper shoeless and rolling her shoulders in sync with the kick drum—she was pretty much the best natural dancer I've ever seen—and when everyone was supposed to shake it like a Polaroid picture, instead they shook it like a bunch of assholes and Harper and I ignored them while I did jazz hands and she played air bass. Looking around I wondered for less than a second if she and I were only together because we despised all the right things. Then she went into a slap-and-pop solo and I realized this was what being in love was: two people protecting each other from a world of idiots.

Harper's dad came and picked us up and we tried to hide how drunk we were and he kept talking about what a nice family the bride came from even if they were a little conservative for his tastes. I tried to agree but I was dizzy and kind of weirdly full and distracted by how much I wanted to get home and sneak into Harper's room and pull off her dress (black) and celebrate that I really did have everything: My girlfriend was sexy and smart and preppy, but almost sardonically preppy in a way genuine snobs were too dense to pick up on. Her dad parked the car at the end of their long driveway and I said I'd be right in and collapsed into their ivy and puked a mix of champagne and scotch and everything that made me sick about the world.

My hands felt cool in the plants and dirt and Harper came back out. I looked up from the ivy. "Harper? I love you as much as I hate Richmond."

She looked up at the stars. "Wow," she said, "you must love me a lot."

LAS VEGAS, Jan. 13 The guy in the cowboy hat at the end of the table rolls nine, which means I get another eight reds. I've asked Keegan to keep track of the money since she's better at math than I am but she insists on calling the chips by their colors instead of their dollar amounts. All we know for sure is that right now I have eight greens on the table and sixteen reds and three blues. I think they add up to about $1,200 but I really have no idea.

"You would think chips are just toys, right?" Keegan breathes hot in my ear, her hand on my arm. I sense the other people around the table checking her out and try to look unstable, threatening.

"Except when you're in a casino they have this value they wouldn't have anywhere else," she says. She's sliding one foot out of her heel as she talks, brushing her calf against mine. "Anywhere else the chips would be worth the pennies they cost to make, but in here they, like, destroy people's lives."

I put two greens on six and eight. I don't understand how craps works, really, except that the safest thing to do is leave a lot of money on the pass line and then play six and eight. I came into the game with two hundred-dollar bills and traded them for chips and everything changed.

"The thing is, even money's just a symbol," Keegan says, finishing a vodka tonic. "It isn't like the material in a dollar is actually worth a dollar. So you come in the casino and they replace this one symbol with this other symbol because they want you to feel okay about parting with your symbols, and you've gotten too attached to the old symbol so they give you new ones. How much less would you have on the table right now if it was actually in cash?"

She still sounds giddy, not slurred. I would quit but I'm not sure if I'm allowed to take my chips before a roll and I'm at that awkward point buzz-wise where I'm not yet proud of my diminished faculties.

"And what money really is is just a symbol of how much a product or service or idea is worth. We're worth, you and I, you know, so many thousands a month. But at the same time isn't that entire system kind of laughable when you consider that you can make more standing at this table for twenty minutes than you could make in a year?"

The guy in the cowboy hat rolls a six and I get another stack of chips. I pick them all up slowly, wondering if the guy with the stick is going to call me "sir," which is the universal sign that you've done something wrong. The guy with the stick doesn't say anything and I drop the chips in my pocket, trying to calculate how much I'm up. I slip my hand into Keegan's.

"Can I buy you a drink worth two hours of a Gringo's employee's life?"

She leans into me. "Only if we can drink it in a hotel room worth — worth — I'm sorry. I was gonna say worth X number of hours in a network employee's life, but I don't know if — one of us makes more."

I squeeze her hand, hold up four greens. "It depends what we're doing."

In the hotel room she says she wants to take a shower because she still feels dirty from the desert. We drove the entire way from Arizona with the top down on her convertible Tomahawk. Her shoulders are burned from wearing a strapless dress, and she didn't realize how hot it was because of the air conditioning and her sunglasses.

We went to Vegas because we wanted to do something fun without the risk of anyone from Gringo's seeing me living beyond a fast-food worker's salary. We were torn between Vegas and L.A., but when we saw it was Friday the thirteenth that clinched it.

When she gets out of the shower I tug away her towel and kiss her against the mirrored closet door, trying to press her red shoulders into the cold glass as slowly as possible so she'll feel the burn disappear. Her toothpaste tastes like cinnamon and I take it as an invitation and move my fingertips from the glass to her skin and then back to the glass to try to feel what she's feeling.

She says "ow" and "stop" while I kiss her deeper into the mirror until finally she punches me and says, "Seriously, ow," and looks at me to say she means it. I must look pathetically apologetic because she laughs and shoves me backward onto the bed, laughing at the solid connection as I hit the mattress. I reach up to pull her on top of me and turn her around. "Wouldn't want to hurt your shoulders."

"So chivalrous of you."

I watch her face in the mirror as I slide into her, slowly, and she closes her eyes and lets out a heavy sigh. She leans forward and pushes down, then pulls away fast, squeezing at the very top before plunging down again and squeezing harder at the bottom. She changes the pace at intervals I can't follow, only opening her eyes to glance back at me in the mirror. I feel embarrassed, like she's winning, and she must feel it, too, because she gets a self-satisfied look like she expects me to come any second. I grab her hips and stop moving altogether, holding us in space just to break her rhythm so I can drive into a hard routine. She lets up, dropping her hands from her thighs to the sheets and falling forward so her wet hair touches my knees. I pull her back by her shoulders and she says "owowow," expecting me to wait or apologize or stop but I don't. She laughs like I've passed some little test and starts touching herself, her hand moving as erratically as her body did before, but at least now I don't need to figure out the pattern. We keep moving until she comes, moaning like she's about to cry, and the sound makes me go faster until I come, too. She heaves forward, her palms landing right above my knees, and we're silent except for the sound of our breath, like something accidental has happened.

This is how it is with her every time, except for the sunburn.

She goes into the bathroom and when she climbs back in bed we make a game of me touching her burned arms as softly as possible and her slapping my hands. Finally she asks if she can ask something, in a small, uncertain whisper that makes my stomach hurt.

"It depends," I say.

"It's about . . . the network's sexual harassment policy."

I wait to say anything because I've been worried she would bring something like this up and I want to make it as hard for her as possible. I press my head into my pillow and try to think of an excuse to turn on the TV, some score or stock that needs monitoring, but I'm handicapped by not caring about those kinds of things.

She says, "Hello?"

"I'm listening," I say. "Harassment policy."

"Yeah."

She sits up and I turn sideways to look at her.

"Did . . . Rich do something?"

"No."

She gets up to get her bag off the desk and the backs of her thighs look like hot gold. She turns around holding two pieces of paper, stapled together. "Basically—" She clears her throat. "Employees are barred from having any inappropriate sexual or romantic relationships with people they supervise."

She crawls back into bed, still holding the policy, and moves on top of me as if it will soften the blow. Her soppy hair falls on my cheeks and I try to look curious instead of sad.

"So you're asking for a demotion?"

She rolls slowly onto her back to lie next to me. Her position feels strategic, like she's looking for some kind of consoling commonality. Despite our differences we can at least appreciate the same ceiling.

"I felt like it would have to be okay for us to date, you know, as long as it was—casual," she says. "But now it's sort of—you know, beyond casual, with fairly regular sleepovers and things."

I rotate my neck like I'm trying to get out a kink. "Okay. So."

"So it's turned into almost, kind of, a relationship. And I know we both feel like the story's the most important thing. I wouldn't want to ruin the story, and I know you don't, as good a job as you're doing."

I don't tell her I'm much more interested in her right now than the story.

"So what do we do?" I'm hoping that by saying "we" I can make this seem mutual, whatever she decides. It feels smart, dispassionate, like something a professional would say. I don't want her to think she means more to me already than the job, both because I don't want to scare her off and because she's sort of my boss.

She rolls back onto me but brushes back her hair so it won't fall on me this time, as if that's too intimate now that we're following policy, or would be if we were wearing clothes.

"I just want," she says, "to make sure we aren't in a relationship."

It feels like a trick question. I look past her eyes to the ceiling, then the wall. She lets her hair fall and props herself up to read. "'Sexual relationships hurt everyone in a company because sex partners may give preferential treatment to one another to the detriment of other workers.'" She's quiet for a second. "It's just . . . I can't honestly say I wouldn't give you preferential treatment."

I let out a breath. It's the first time in all this she's sort of said she likes me. I brush a hand through her hair.

"I don't think you can control your thoughts," I say. "You can say it's not a relationship, but does that mean it's not?"

The mascara mottled around her eyes makes everything feel French, black-and-white, doomed. What I'm really asking is for her to say again that she likes me. She looks down at me for a long time.

"You seem like you're mad."

"Mad? Not me."

I look at her like I have no idea why she would think so. But of course I am.

"Because I'm not saying we can't have sex," she says. "I'm just saying it's not a relationship."

I sit up. "I'm sorry?"

She lies back. "That seems the least complicated way."

I glance at myself in the mirror to see how I seem to be reacting. "So what we're doing is . . . what?"

She makes a pained sound and turns onto her stomach. I look at myself, remember I'm an adult now, far out of college, and that I always expected to have complex adult conversations like this.

"I don't know. I guess we're—I don't know." She sounds embarrassed.

I turn back toward her. "So we're basically—are we—fucking?"

She twists her mouth, blinks at me as if adjusting to the light. "If you have to put it in the most disgusting possible terms, yes."

"I guess I'd be pretty stupid to complain about a beautiful girl saying she wants no strings attached." I leave room for her to say something but she doesn't. "That's what I'm supposed to want, right?"

She half-smiles. I want to think it's a regretful look, that she wants more, but she just turns over on her side. I feel outmaneuvered. We don't talk for so long I think she's asleep, until she says, "I think I just need a disco nap."

I get up and turn out the lights. "Are we going to dinner?"

"Yeah," she says. "But you can't buy. That would be too much like a relationship."

I climb back into bed, facing away from her, wondering if our bodies can touch or if that would be too involved. When I think she's asleep she reaches across me so she's holding my hand and I sigh a satisfied sigh to let her know this will all somehow be okay. A few minutes go by in the dark and she whispers, her voice small and soft, "Why did that Maria girl wink at you?"

TEMPE, Ariz. Jan. 16 Maria comes up behind me as I'm mopping and says I'm getting the lyrics wrong. I'm singing the Smashing Pumpkins song that came on satellite radio last night on the ride home from Vegas. I thought the words were "despite all my rage I am still just a retina cage," but Maria says it's actually "rat in a cage."

"What do your words even mean?" she says. "Who's ever heard of a retina cage?"

"I don't know." I put the mop in the bucket. "I was thinking of like a cage for eyes."

"How do you cage eyes? He's a rat in a cage. How do I know the words better than you when that song's like however many years old and I'm only nineteen?"

I'm suddenly too distracted to explain. Nineteen-year-olds are kind of like adults. I don't have to feel bad anymore about checking her out, not that I can get away with it too often.

My glasses are a retina cage.

Ann and Hanlon and, of course, Rich would accept that occasionally in a typical workday the ass of one's co-worker might happen into view. But Keegan isn't likely to buy it, especially after what she asked in Vegas. I pretended to be asleep and that I didn't hear her, but it gave me a minor thrill, the idea that she might be jealous of some other girl winking at me. Then I felt guilty at enjoying the thought because what kind of asshole can't even commit to a girl who wants no commitment?

Maria says to put the mop in the closet because Frank wants her to show me something. Everything she says now feels fraught with double meanings and I try to re-imagine it in the most suggestive way possible, in the worst way Keegan could possibly interpret it. I hope Maria's smile will come off on video as condescending and not flirtatious and that what she shows me will be completely work-related. I wheel the bucket to the back, with her walking three steps ahead of me, and I don't look even once at her ass or her hair, which looks really good today.

When I've put the mop and bucket in the closet she leads me back out to the drive-thru counter. She puts on a wireless headset but pushes its microphone away from her mouth.

"We don't have to talk anymore," she says.

"Excuse me?"

"We don't talk anymore. People pull up to the sign and they talk to an operator instead of us. Then the operator sends the order by instant message."

She points to a blank screen to the left of the window where the orders are supposed to appear.

"Where's the operator?"

"I don't know," she says. "Jamaica."

I've read about this: drive-thru outsourcing.

"Do they get the orders right?"

Maria adjusts her headset. "Frank says we get way less complaints now."

"Can we hear the orders?"

"Yeah," she says. "That's why we wear the headsets. But don't bother talking because they can't hear you."

She pulls a headset from a drawer and passes it to me. As I switch it on, a low rumble comes though the headphones. The sound of a car engine. The next thing I hear is the baritone of the operator, inviting and Jamaican.

"Good morning to you," he says to the customer, "and welcome to Gringo's."

"Well. Thank you so much." The voice is female, delighted.

"Thank you for coming," the operator says. "We realize how many choices you have and appreciate your business. Now tell me this: How may I serve you today?"

"Oh." She sounds like she's forgotten why she's here. "Could I have just an Eggrito, no cheese, and a . . . coffee?"

"And will that be with cream and sugar?"

"Um," she says. "Is it possible it could be . . . black?"

I look at Maria: Does this seem weird to her? She's picking skull decals off her nails.

"Of course," the operator laughs.

The customer laughs, too. There's an awkward pause I interpret as sexual tension.

"Let me ask you this frankly," the operator says. "Do you think I can interest you today in one of our delicious southwestern hash browns or a minirito with your Eggrito and black coffee? It's always good to have something extra to get through the day."

"Maybe so." The customer is practically purring. "Is there one that you can . . . recommend?"

"Both are simply astonishing."

A breathy whisper: "Surprise me."

"There's but one more thing I need to ask," the operator asks. "What would you like for dessert? I would recommend an ice cream taco."

"This early in the morning?"

"With all due respect, miss, it's expected to be eighty-one degrees in the Phoenix area today. Very hot for January."

"Okay," the customer says. "I'm in your hands."

From her voice I'm guessing it's been a while since anyone called her miss. It's a calculated risk by the Jamaican that pays off huge.

"Anything else, my dear?"

The customer pauses, dares herself to go on.

"Only—well—has anyone ever told you that you should be on the radio? Your voice is so . . . soulful."

The Jamaican's laughter booms. "Thank you," he says. "Perhaps someday. If you promise to call in and talk to me."

She laughs. "I'll see *you* at the window."

Maria goes around the corner to get the customer's food from the kitchen. I'm left standing by the window as the customer pulls up in her Accord, smiling expectantly. She has deep laugh lines and a short unfussy haircut, brown hair turning grey. She looks past me with flashing blue eyes, scanning the restaurant, then turns to me as her smile disappears.

"Where's the guy who took my order?" she says.

I look back at her, then at the floor. I feel like part of a con.

"He's, um, not here?"

She glares at me. "I'd like to speak to your manager."

Frank is walking toward the front of the restaurant and hears her as he passes. He brushes past me to lean out the window.

"Good morning, ma'am, what can I do for you?"

She points at me. "This employee just took my order, and he was doing . . . a voice."

Frank looks at me, already resigned to disappointment. "Really," he says. "What kind of voice?"

Maria comes around the corner with the food and leaves again to get the coffee.

"He was doing . . . a *black* voice," the customer says. "And I know it was him because the only other one with a headset is the girl."

Frank looks at me again. "A black voice."

"You know," the woman says. "Kind of . . . deep, and really like, you know."

Frank leans out the window. "Deep, and kind of low?"

"Right," the woman says. "And you know, dropping the g's at the ends of each word—"

"Kind of slangy," Frank says. "Inarticulate."

I glare at him. "Isn't that sort of a generalization?'"

"You're the one who did it," the customer snaps at me. She turns back to Frank. "He was doing this awful routine, like, 'Let me *serve* you.'"

"Step and fetchit," Frank says. "'Right away, massa.'"

"It was mixed in with kind of an island patois, totally over-the-top and exaggerated. And he was flirting with me, also. Or trying to. You know that whole stereotype of the black man as some kind of purely sexual being—"

"Right, trying to get with the white women," Frank says. "Jungle fever."

"The whole Mandingo thing."

"I'm the black stud. Et cetera."

"Hey, white lady, I've got some blacksnake here for you in my pants. Want to see this pantsnake?"

I interrupt. "What the fuck?"

"Say my name," Frank says. "Say it, whitebread."

"Luther," the customer says. "No, Tyrone."

"That's right, crackerbarrel. Tyrone's got somethin' for you."

The customer closes her eyes. "Give it to me, Tyrone."

"Yessum, Miss cracker lady."

"Right," the customer says. "That's *exactly* what he was doing." She straightens up in her seat.

"The worst part about it," she says, "is that today is Martin Luther King Day."

It's true. The bus schedules were all messed up this morning.

"Really shameful," Frank says. "On the day we're supposed to be colorblind—"

Maria arrives with the coffee and takes the woman's money, which she passes to Frank.

"I cannot tell you how sorry I am," Frank says, leaning so far out the window he has to hold the frame to support himself. "We could not be more committed to diversity here at Gringo's. I myself am a second-generation Mexican-American, and cannot tell you how much Dr. King's legacy speaks to me, as I think it speaks to all Americans."

I feel a hard kick to the shin. The customer closes her eyes and gives a deep R&B nod.

"Mmm-hmmm."

I feel another kick and glance down too late to catch Frank's foot on camera. He looks at me again, his jaw clenched, and I realize I'm supposed to say something, too.

"Um," I say. "I just, wow. I cannot say how sorry I am. I just—learned? I just learned such an incredible . . . lesson from both of you. Wow. I mean, thanks."

The customer looks at me skeptically. "I hope so," she says. She and Frank share one last soulful look and she drives away.

"Seriously," I say, "why couldn't we just say the operator's in Jamaica?"

Frank's eyes stare blankly into mine. He looks exhausted.

"We don't advertise that to customers," he says. "Would it be so hard to just say it was you and apologize? You know the first rule of customer service, right?"

I try to remember the GRAND system.

"Greet the customer?"

"No, Scott. The customer is always right."

I feel my face going into a scowl. "What if the customer is totally wrong?" I say. "I didn't say any of those things."

He moves closer, momentarily furious, and then the anger seems to go out of him. He shakes his head and walks out. Maria passes him, coming back in.

"Look," she says, "the drive-thru's a touchy subject. The same thing used to happen to Gary."

Finally, some background on racist Gary. I lean a little closer to make sure she's on mic.

"What used to happen to Gary?"

She pushes back her bangs with her headset. "He wanted those jobs to go to people here," she says. "Americans."

"White Americans?"

"Yeah," she says. "And, you know, black Americans and Asian-Americans and illegal Mexicans. People in our borders. Americans."

The day is a total loss. At the end of the shift I have to walk two extra blocks to Mill Avenue to catch a bus that runs past Keegan's hotel. I'm almost at the stop, looking out at a billboard for a movie about a child rapist, when I realize I never saw Frank put the customer's money in the cash register.

LOS ANGELES, Jan. 21 The guy in the Prius to my left keeps honking and I turn to yell at my closed window that it isn't going to help. He stares back at me through the glass so I roll it down.

"That's right, Sun Devil. I'm honking at you," the guy says. "Here's honking at you, Sun Devil."

The guy looks small in his seat, wearing Malcolm X glasses and a Paul Frank shirt I think I have myself.

"Me?"

"Yeah, you. I saw your license plate, Sun Devil."

Keegan and I each bought Arizona State license-plate holders for our respective Tomahawks to cheer ourselves out of some recent hangover. They say "Fork 'Em Devils" and have the ASU mascot holding a little pitchfork. The concierge found us a screwdriver so we could put them on our cars.

"What, you root for UCLA or something? Because I don't really care. Whatever. Go Bruins."

"No," he says. "I root for Cal, Sun Devil. Go Golden Bears. And FYI, you don't need to leave your engine idling the entire time we're parked here. If you haven't noticed, we aren't moving."

I drove here from Arizona when it was still dark, hoping to avoid the typical Saturday afternoon clusterfuck. But of course it was a mess from the 10 all the way to the corner of Sunset and Gower, where we've been trapped for twenty minutes behind a flipped-over police car. I zoned out and forgot to turn off my engine.

"Yeah," I say. "Well."

"Yeah," he says. "That's right. You know, if you want to run your car all the time you might think about getting one that gets better than nineteen miles per gallon."

He keeps staring. I can see his anger building with each passing second and the way his lip twists makes me laugh inadvertently.

"Oh, it's funny?" He's yelling now. "You think you can come into *my* state driving a *socially unconscious vehicle* disguised as a sedan and just laugh? Not enough for you people to pollute your own air? Congratulations on your real estate market going to shit, by the way. That's what you get for overbuilding. Do me a favor and don't ruin my state, too."

There are so many things I could say: that I read the same *Times* article he did about Phoenix real estate, and that things aren't as bad as it said; that Arizona's air quality may be the sixteenth worst in the country, but that L.A.'s is the worst; that I have a hybrid just like his in my parking space a few miles ahead. But just as I'm about to start yelling statistics I see that they've loaded the cop car on a flatbed and that it's pulling away, so what I yell instead is, "Fuck you, shitface!" and pull away.

Two hours later I'm climbing the slope toward Wineglass' sculpture garden, wearing a Batman mask to thwart the hidden cameras. I brush past scrub or whatever these types of sharp scraggly trees are called, except I can't really say because I'm not one of those people who knows the names of trees. I think I'm moving up the west side of the Wineglass estate except I'm not one of those people who always knows east from west either, and it's starting to drizzle but I tell myself the only way to get something like this done is methodically, one square foot at a time, without skipping any sections.

I remember one of my first stories at the network, going out with a team of hunters to search the Ohio-West Virginia state line for signs of that summer's missing blond girl. The local sheriff or firefighters or whoever had put out a call for hunters because they were supposed to know the land best. I crawled out on my hands and knees, shoulder-to-shoulder with the hunters, so I could report back from the ground on the search conditions. We were supposed to look for bullet fragments, locks of hair, clothes—the sheriff's deputies had made a list of things they imagined us finding—and I hoped I wouldn't be the one to find anything because I was supposed to report the story, not be part of it.

As much as I wanted the hunters to conform to my stereotypes—heartless, bloodthirsty—they were the friendliest guys you'd ever hope to meet. They kept saying that after we found the girl I should come back and they'd take me hunting again, but this time for bucks instead of child remnants. We didn't find anything except shells from the previous year's hunt (which were tagged and identified as belonging to "the good guys"). That night at the VFW hall Rich and I got some good interviews where everyone kept using the word "heartsick" and referred to the girl by her first name (Amanda, I think) whether they knew her or not. After we filed our story I drank beers with the hunters and promised I'd come back to hunt for bucks though of course I never did. I asked them to please call my cell if they heard anything about the search that the police weren't saying. It turned out later the girl had just run away, to Los Angeles, where she had joined the most successful of the city's religions.

I try to search for the ring the same way we searched for the girl, one square foot at a time, except I'm the only one searching and it's starting to rain, and I probably haven't planned this out as well as I should have. I start my search about forty feet back from where the canyon starts the sharp incline up to Wineglass' property, so I'm looking up about one hundred feet to the giraffe. I stay alert for distant flashes of something shiny but I know the light catching the ring while I'm looking for it would take the kind of luck I don't deserve.

I search for half an hour before it starts to rain for real, and part of me knows I'm going to give myself permission to give up. And then I hear voices up near the giraffe.

I make out three figures, the one on the left holding a flashlight and the one on the right carrying an honest-to-God lantern that has to be dramatic effect. In their other hands I make out what can only be shotguns. I recognize the man in the middle as Wineglass, who cups his hands around his mouth and calls out—I'm not making this up—"State your business."

It takes the rest of the afternoon to remind him who I am and why I'm here. He's surprisingly understanding about the mask and says he, too, prefers not to be photographed. He promises his help finding the ring, and I agree to send him a full description of it, complete with pictures from the Canadian company that sold it to me, just in case more than one ring turns up in his canyon. I think I'm free to go but he has a question I'm not expecting:

"What kind of stories are you working on?"

TEMPE, Ariz., Jan. 23 I get a five a.m. wake-up call to Keegan's room on most of the mornings I have to go to Gringo's, but on the occasional nights I stay at the network apartment to confuse her I wake up to Bloc Party on the CD alarm singing about people who don't read the papers and don't read the news.

Whichever place I wake up on Gringo's days, I always have an acidic feeling in my gut, like this is the day I'm going to get caught. It goes away when I put on the glasses and tell myself this isn't my real life. But by the time I've run the wires to the flash deck in the fanny pack the acidic feeling has come back because if this isn't my real life, then what is?

Even without the wires it would take longer to get ready for work at Gringo's than at the network because at Gringo's they actually care if I shave and comb my hair. Before I head out the door I make a quick check of e-mail to make sure there's no progress in Ferndekamp getting a confirmation hearing and no word on Carlotta Espinoza giving her story to another news outlet with standards less exacting than ours. I catch the 5:28 bus if I'm at Keegan's or walk to work if I'm at the apartment, and try as a personal challenge to get to Gringo's ten minutes early. I'm filled with a sense of minor accomplishment if I make it, a sense that I'm sort of in control and that everything is simplified now. My only task is to do my job, or actually both of my jobs: working at Gringo's and recording myself working at Gringo's.

In the minutes I wait for Frank to show I always question myself about whether watching is enough. I tell myself anyone can watch—that reporters have to ask questions, push issues, dig. But then I wonder how much I can ask and push and dig before what I'm doing turns into entrapment, and tell myself I don't want to make people do things they wouldn't do otherwise. I wonder how Ann and Hanlon would weigh in but I know that if I asked, they would look at me strangely and say to just be as fair as possible, as if I should have known that much without having to ask.

One of the cars coming down the street will finally turn out to be Frank's and as he makes his way to the door he never asks how long I've been waiting. I spend the first hour or so with Juan and Carlos, prepping food, wondering why they haven't been singing their little song lately and if asking them to sing would be unfair or suspicious. By the time it seems like they're in a singing mood Frank will come in like he's been looking for me for hours and announce that I'm supposed to be trained in some new task. He'll tell me to go out front and mop until Maria arrives to do the training, but Maria never comes in before nine, even when she's due at eight. While I mop I catch myself thinking about what jeans she'll be wearing and whether she'll have had time to do her hair, and about the rule I read about in one of Harper's old magazines that says a woman can date anyone within ten years of her age as long as she's at least twenty and he's at least eighteen. I subtract ten from twenty-nine, then thirty-nine, then forty-nine, until the difference in years seems smaller and smaller.

The days when Maria shows up wearing low-rise jeans or capris seem to go a little faster, and I always think we'll be able to bond over training but we never do because she always seems too tired to talk about anything except being tired. The tasks I'm trained on, from washing windows to ordering new lettuce, are never interesting enough to sustain me through the day, much less provide more than B-roll for our soon-to-be-nationally televised investigative piece about the prospective secretary of labor. After another round of mopping I'll finally feel brave or bored enough to go into the back rooms to ask questions and force issues but by then it's time to leave.

Sometimes when I get to Keegan's for the one p.m. teleconference there's been some worrisome rumor about a Ferndekamp hearing or new anxiety over Carlotta Espinoza. On these days Keegan is a ball of stress, stomping around the room in her boots of the non-sexy variety. When the teleconference starts I'll summarize my day into the speakerphone as Keegan and I review my day's footage and relay it to Ann and Hanlon and Rich in New York. They'll say things like "hmm" or "that doesn't sound too eventful," but Ann will reassure us that everything's fine, that we're still basically at the stage where I'm gaining the trust of the people I'm secretly covering. She'll say she's sure I'll get some great stuff soon enough, but could I please make sure to pay especially close attention tomorrow?

Then there are days when Keegan's had nothing to worry about all morning, and she'll open her door in a bathrobe, a drowsy look in her eyes and new nail polish on her toes. Before the teleconference I'll pull the fuzzy belt from her robe and tie her wrists to the headboard of her bed and as soon as we've punched in our code for the conference call and said our hellos with New York I'll go down on her, licking patiently at first and then using something from a *Men's Journal* article I read at the gym: During oral sex stiffen your tongue and use the tip like a pen to write the alphabet on the woman's clitoris. The article says this is a good way to keep focus, and to switch to numbers when you run out of letters, but my personal variation is to skip the numbers and go from the alphabet into entire sentences like *Please come Keegan,* or *I'll show you who's boss,* or *What if I don't want to keep things casual?*

Ann will tell us about the latest Ferndekamp speculation or Rich will mumble about another "promising" disclosure from his secret source and I'll write on Keegan with increasing pressure and urgency, cajoling and pleading until she breaks down and buries her face sideways in her pillows so no one in New York can hear her come.

TEMPE, Ariz., Jan. 30 In the kitchen I have to keep myself from laughing when Frank introduces me to the new hire, not just because his glasses are even worse than mine but also because his name is Julio. Julio is a pretty suave, lady-killing kind of name but this guy looks as mal-adjusted as you can imagine, with acne clusters and a horrible ponytail he's tucked into the back of his collar in an apparent attempt at looking professional. If I can't win this guy over as a friend I'm hopeless.

"So Julio here is going to maybe show you today how to use the fryer," Frank says. "I know it's a little awkward since Julio has actually been working here less time than you, but yesterday Juan and Carlos showed him the basics and now he's just got it down cold. Or hot. Since it's a fryer. That thing is hot."

Julio nods and Frank claps him on the back. I can tell Frank's trying to play us off each other, to make me improve out of jealousy, but I refuse to let myself be managed. I need as many friends on the inside as I can get and I'm not going to let Frank mess things up with an easy mark like Julio.

"Now before Julio can make you a *master* of the fryer I need you to *master* another system. Do you want to guess what it's called?"

I shrug.

"I just gave you two hints," Frank says.

I shrug again. After the drive-thru debacle I refuse to use words like "master."

Frank hands me a pamphlet for a new system called MAST and starts to run through what each of the letters stands for. I kind of zone out but think he says the T is for temperature. Frank says as an experiment he's going to have Julio teach me as we go along instead of having me read the pamphlet.

"I'm getting the sense," Frank says, "that you're more an *experiential* than visual learner." He says "experiential" very slowly.

Frank leaves us alone and Julio looks at me for the first time. "All right," he says. "Let's fry some churros."

Churros are part of the reason I was so fat in fourth grade. We used to eat them on field trips to the zoo or Fisherman's Wharf, where old Mexican women sold them from carts where they rotated on skewers like hot dogs. They're pieces of long dough, star-shaped at the ends, and dipped in sugar or cinnamon or both before they're warmed over. I won't find out all the steps involved in making them while I'm working here because the churros we're supposed to deep-fry have already been rolled and dipped and shipped to us, frozen.

"Okay," Julio says. "This should be pretty easy."

I smile attentively. I'm trying to keep things simple. I wonder why he's working here at almost my age but figure his story will come out soon enough. For now the best thing is to listen, do what he says, and earn his respect as a reliable colleague.

"We fry these and use them as a base for the ingredients in a Classic Churrito," he says. His tone is easy, cheerful, like he realizes the ridiculousness of what we're doing and seems more amused than offended that this is his job. "I don't know how a Classic Churrito is different from a regular churrito, but maybe they'll tell us later."

It takes me a minute to realize he's joking. I hadn't expected him to be the one to break the ice. Good for him.

"Yeah," I say.

"Okay," he says. "So we basically take six or eight of these at a time, thaw them in the microwave"—he works as he does it—"which is the first step in MAST, by the way—microwave. Are you getting this?"

I look up from the clump of frozen churros. He broke off exactly six at once and I don't understand how he's learned to do this so quickly.

"Yeah," I say. "Microwave."

He grins with surprising confidence. I had expected him to be kind of a nebbish.

"So then we load the basket," he says, moving the churros there from the microwave, "and—oh, snap. I forgot a step."

I look at him, unsure how to help.

"Activate fryer," he says. "The second part of MAST."

I laugh. "Right."

He flips a switch on the fryer, turns a dial.

"In a Classic Churrito," he says, "the churro is surrounded with sour cream, cheese, black beans, and meat, all wrapped in a flour tortilla. We don't have to make them right now. This is just FYI."

Now I'm a little intimidated. A light comes on to indicate the fryer is working.

"So, okay," Julio says. "We've loaded the basket, and now we do the next step—'Start frying.'"

He lowers the basket into simmering vegetable oil and moves to the counter across from the fryer. He leans against it and waits.

"So," he says. "What's your prescription?"

I look at the basket. He wants me to diagnose the churros?

"Um," I say. "Good?"

He looks at me like I'm to be pitied, tries again. "Nearsighted or farsighted?"

So he means my glasses. The only problem is that in real life my vision's perfect and I have no idea what I'm pretending to be.

"Um, near."

"Yeah," he says. "Me, too. I'm like 20/80. Really bad."

"Yeah," I say. "I'm like, 20/500."

His tilts his head. "Isn't that legally blind?"

"Hey," I say, feeling my face turn red. "Should we check the temperature?"

"What?"

"The last step. T is for Temperature."

He pushes his glasses up on his nose. "No," he says. "T is for Taste."

"Oh," I say. "You're sure?"

"Yeah," he says. "T is for Temperature in the STAC system. Not in MAST. In MAST we taste. Except Frank said it's optional. I kind of think they just add it so that it will spell MAST instead of MAS."

We're kindred spirits. I wish I were making a better impression.

"Hey," he says. "Let me try your glasses on."

My hands start to shake and I put them in my pockets. "Should we, uh, check the temperature anyway? To make sure it's cooking hot enough?"

He looks at the basket. "If it's bubbling like that, it's boiling."

"Do you know that from STAC? Or from MAST?"

He stares at me. "I know," he says, "because that's what boiling is. Let me try on your glasses."

He steps toward me and I step back.

"I don't think so," I say. "It's so . . . personal."

He holds out his hand. "Come on," he says, his face a semi-scowl. "It's not."

"No, really," I say. "It's like voting."

If he pulls the glasses off my face it will also pull the wires and tape out of my shirt and then things will be really awkward. I hold onto the frames with both hands so he can't get them but he says, "Come on, man, be cool" and reaches out to grip the top of the frames, above my nose, right where the camera is. He tugs on the frame and I say, "Dude, come on" in a weak voice. There's no time to do anything else so I snap off the right earpiece of the glasses, the one with no wires in it. He lets go.

"Shit, dude." I let the glasses hang from their strap, keeping the wires concealed. "Seriously."

Julio turns back to the fryer and lifts out the churros. He's quite the multi-tasker. He says "oh, damn," in a tone that doesn't convey actual disappointment and turns back to me, holding out his hand. "Let me see," he says. "I can fix them."

"No you can't," I say. "They're a little harder to fix than you realize, which is why you maybe shouldn't break things you can't pay to have fixed."

He looks hurt. "Whatever you say, Mr. Rich Folks."

I step back in case he tries to grab them from around my neck. "That's not what I'm saying. I'm working here the same as you. But I'm saying you can't just screw them back together. It's really hard."

"I told you I'll fix them." He turns a dial on the fryer.

"Just . . . taste the churros," I say. "I'm going to the bathroom."

"Whatever."

I guess we aren't going to be friends.

I go to the bathroom to disconnect myself, pulling off all the tape and wires and wrapping them around the glasses, then shoving the whole mess in the fanny pack. I don't know how long it will take to fix the glasses. I'll have to spend the rest of the day squinting and pretending I can't see. Ann will say I should have handled the situation differently, and with hours to think about it someone at the network will be able to tell me how.

I look in the mirror and see myself in a Gringo's shirt and no glasses for the first time. It occurs to me that tomorrow, without my hidden camera, I'll be like any other Gringo's employee, working without watching.

Tomorrow is off the record.

TEMPE, Ariz., Jan. 31 "If you could be a little less polite to people, I can't even tell you how much it would help."

"Of course, of course."

"And—see, right there—when you say 'Of course,' don't say it so benevolently, like you're a king or something. Act like you're bored. Just say, 'Sure, right,' almost to the point that people wonder if you're even paying attention to them."

"I don't know about that. Why is it wrong to be pleasant to people?"

"It's not wrong. It's great. It's just, when you do it at a restaurant like this—they get suspicious."

We've gone at least twenty minutes without a customer so the Jamaican and I have been talking through the drive-thru speaker outside. He says his name is Luke, which I'm sure is fake, but he insists it isn't. I try to think about what kind of name I think a Jamaican guy should have and all I can come up with is Bob, which makes me feel ashamed.

"Okay," Luke says. "I'll try it. But if it fails to work I'm going back to politeness."

"Deal," I say. "And Luke, please. Promise me you'll look into unionizing."

He asked a few minutes into our conversation how much we get paid here and it turns out we make three times what he does, even though he regularly works twelve-hour days. He's one of forty people at his call center, handling orders from restaurants across the U.S. I told him he should at least be getting medical and dental.

Luke laughs a deep, hopeless laugh.

"Unionizing," he says. "Right."

I wouldn't dream of giving him advice if the glasses were on, but Keegan sent them back to New York this morning to be fixed. I tell him I should get back to work.

"Me, too," he says. "And remember: be grateful for what you have."

I say I am, and not to be weirded out if I act different the next time we talk—people in America are watched all the time. Then I go inside and almost bump into Maria at the GRAND door.

"Hey," she says. "Frank wants to talk to you."

Without the glasses and the risk of anyone at the network losing respect for me, I'm willing to be more of a supplicant today than usual. I walk down the hall, interested in seeing Frank's office for the first time, and resolve to rebuild his impression of me.

The office is smaller than I expected, and Frank sits behind a desk facing toward the door. Stacks of coupon booklets sit new and unused in front of him. Fifty cents off a Sushirito, thirty-five cents off a Peruviano. The shelves behind him are full of files and books. I count three titles about leadership. There's a full-sized computer monitor on his desk, and for a moment I pity Frank for his old equipment. Then I notice the TV behind him.

The image on the screen is split into four sections, each showing a different part of the restaurant, including the drive-thru. A shelf above the TV has videotapes labeled with the days of the week, except for Tuesday.

Today.

Without looking at me Frank hits a button on a remote. He rewinds and I see minutes-old footage of myself at the drive-thru speaker.

"There's no sound," Frank says, looking from the monitor to me. "Mind telling me what you were talking about?"

My first instinct is to say I was talking to myself, but that would only add to his initial drug suspicion. With no time for anything better I go for the truth—that I was trying to get Luke to sound more American. I leave out the part about telling him to unionize.

Frank makes a circle on the desk with his thumb.

"So you thought, basically, you could just go out there and have a little chat with the operator and improve our entire system?"

He seems skeptical that someone would do such a thing for the good of the company.

"We were talking about . . . his diction." I swallow, remind myself that the glasses aren't on and that no one else will hear me. "And also about the situation the other day, which was entirely my fault."

Frank leans back in his chair, leather. I think from his expression that he may be impressed.

"Well," he says. "I hope you taught him something. Just do me a favor and ask next time before you do that."

He looks me in the eye, waiting for the nod, and I give it eagerly, grateful to get off so easy. He turns to the TV and hits the remote again, showing us real-time shots of the counter, drive-thru, drive-thru booth, and kitchen. The system is for checking on employees, not customers.

Frank says, "Watch this," and holds down a button. The camera at the counter slowly zooms in on a shot of Maria, standing sideways. Frank maneuvers the camera to her legs and leans toward the monitor as if nothing could be more arousing than the poorly lit, grainy shot of what could be anything. He looks at me like an animal trying to determine if I'm one of its kind.

"Wow," I say.

He nods. "Do you see how close I'm watching Maria right now?"

"Yeah," I say. I wish I was recording this.

He pulls back on the zoom to show her tapping her hands on the register.

"I want you to watch her that close, too," Frank says. "Learn to do what she does. Following instructions. Being at her station. Not causing trouble with customers."

I nod, try to make my eyes bigger.

"Okay," he says. "Go tell her you're gonna be her shadow today. And shut the door behind you."

At the counter, I try to stand between Maria and the camera.

"So are you going to literally shadow me?" she says. "Like stand right there all day?"

"I can stand off to the side," I say. "But I should stay close because Frank said he'd be checking on us."

I say it as a test, to see if she knows about the camera system. The way she exhales suggests she does. Her bangs blow up from her face, then fall back down as she offers me a coffee.

She steps back to show me the twenty-ounce cup she's hidden under the counter, next to the bags and trays, in clear violation of the sanitation section of the STAC pamphlet. I guess she knows what rules can be bent. I say no thanks, and she takes a sip and goes back to tapping the sides of the register, sighing like she wishes there was something better to do with all her caffeinated energy.

I see gothic lettering on the inside of her right wrist and ask what it is. She holds it up, looking surprised and happy someone's noticed.

"I drew it," she says.

It's the word "Olivia" written in 12-point calligraphic script. She's pretty good and I hope it's not some kind of gang thing.

"You're left-handed?"

"No."

I nod to show I'm impressed.

"Who's Olivia?"

Maria licks her thumb and tries to rub away some smudge below the tip of the V pointing toward her palm.

"She's my daughter," she says. "She'll be one in two weeks."

"Nice," I say. "Congratulations."

She smiles like she's discovered some new perk: she gets to celebrate two birthdays.

"I told my mom as a joke I wanted Olivia's name as a tattoo, but my mom said not in her house. So I've been drawing it on in the morning to freak her out."

I glance up at the camera and adjust where I'm standing to make sure Frank's view is still blocked.

"You live with your mom?"

She blows her bangs upward again. I've hit a bad topic.

"I'm moving out," Maria says.

I wait a respectful millisecond before asking, "With Olivia's dad?"

"Well, it's . . . I don't know," she says. "It's a long story."

I don't say anything.

"Me and Olivia's dad," she says, "aren't really on the best terms right now."

She looks in my eyes and I recognize her expression as the same one women always have when I interview them about their husbands or boyfriends going to Iraq. Of course reporters always promote boyfriends to fiancés if they die but this is the kind of lie everyone wants. What the women object to is when you act like everything will turn out great. There's nothing more condescending than fake optimism.

"I'm sorry," I say.

"It's for the best," she says.

I feel a moment of elation at the thought that she might really be done with the guy, then think: Why would that make me happy? I spend a few seconds lying to myself that I'm glad no girl this bright is still with a guy dumb enough to get her pregnant this young. But of course the thing I'm actually thinking is that I'm glad she's theoretically available.

I catch myself and feel guilty, but then, what benefits do fast-food workers get besides daydreams? I let myself wonder. What if I didn't have the glasses and fanny pack? If I stayed in Arizona and both of us did our best and got promoted? What if we went out for a drink some night and complained about customers and ended up making out? Could that ever happen? Would I meet Olivia? What if we ended up really liking each other? Could we afford to move in together? Could we survive? I don't know how to be a regular person. Could I do what people call an honest day's work and then come home and blog about my day? Would my thoughtful observations about life in the working class attract the attention of NPR? Would they occasionally call me for a real person's perspective on life in the trenches? Would my Hispanic girlfriend add to my credibility?

Maria touches her hair. I notice the smallness of her hands and feel guilty again. A few minutes ago I was disgusted at Frank for zooming in on her, but I would probably do the same thing if I had a clearer picture and a better angle.

"Hey." Frank swings open the GRAND door. "I spilled something in my office."

He stands there and I look at him like I'm waiting for his punchline. Then I remember: Frank's messes are my problem.

"Sure," I say. "I'll get the mop."

I walk down the hall to his office. There's a puddle next to his desk of something that smells like root beer. I slap the mop into it and then look up at the monitor. The screen shows him behind the register with Maria, alone.

I see him reach into the register and pull out some bills, then slide them into her back pocket. He whispers something, leaving his hand on her ass. She stands frozen, staring straight ahead without objecting, as if his touching her is part of their deal. He's paying partly for the method of payment, like a guy sliding money into a g-string.

I mop up the root beer or whatever it is and wonder if Frank spilled it on purpose just to get me out of the way. He hands Maria one of the coupon stacks that were on his desk—this is his idea of a tip?—and pats her ass again before walking out of the frame.

If I can catch him on video I can keep him from touching her again. I can save her, not in the self-serving way customers want to save strippers, but in a new, unselfish way that doesn't involve having sex with her.

Not that I wouldn't.

NEW YORK, Feb. 3 The transcription people have outdone themselves. They always get words wrong, but this is the first time I've caught them making things up.

"We need to fix this," I tell Rich. "Frank did make me apologize to the woman at the drive-thru, but he never called me a 'fucking asshole,' or as they've spelled it, a 'fuckling asfhole.' And he never said, quote, 'If that happens again they'll find your bvomes drying in the desert.' And what are bvomes? Bones? Watch the video. Never happened."

Rich comes out from behind his desk and I'm horrified to see that he's barefoot. He walks across the faux polar bear rug and before I can think of an escape he engulfs me in the wool of his turtleneck, smothering me as I lie that I have a cold. Everything in his office is winter white, from the bear beneath our feet to his sweater to his leather recliner. This isn't his real office, just the one he uses when he's on the East Coast. His real office, in Burbank, is lit entirely with candles.

I flew out after yesterday's Gringo's shift to get fitted for new glasses and compare notes with Rich on what I have from the ground and what he's getting from his source on high. I especially want to know if any of the higher-ups at Gringo's have figured out Frank is pocketing money from the register. My theory is that Ferndekamp has such a laissez-faire approach to regulating his restaurants that Frank is able to not only sexually exploit one of his employees but also pay her off with money that rightfully belongs to Gringo's. Even if shareholders don't care about the harassment, they'll care about the money. And our viewers will have to wonder if someone who oversees all these problems should be secretary of labor.

Rich releases me from the hug and walks around his desk, gesturing for me to take one of the space-age plastic chairs for guests. He puts his feet up.

"You can't get too worked up about typos," Rich says. "People are imperfect. They're just doing their jobs."

He's trying to bait me into overreacting so he can seem like the cool one. It's the same thing with the polar bear rug. He wants to provoke global warming people into objecting to the pseudo-murder of their movement's mascot so he can sputter and shake his head: What? People aren't allowed to have rugs now? It just feels nice on bare feet. Where are we going as a society when fake bears have more rights than people?

I try to sound as bored as possible. "I think writing lines for Frank goes a little beyond the transcription service's responsibilities," I say. "But anyway, the money. Did you get to ask about it? If Frank has some deal where he's allowed to keep money from the register, great. But if not—"

He puts his feet on the floor and opens his laptop, a hopeful sign. We may actually accomplish something today.

"Here's the thing," he says, looking at me empathetically. "We need to talk about narrative."

He spins the laptop around to show me a web site with photos of a blonde woman, topless and blindfolded. A hairy, bald guy is touching her nose with a banana.

"See, easy gimmick here. Normally this guy could never get this girl. But add a blindfold—"

"Rich. Did you even ask your source? Seriously. I have to get back for a shift Monday."

He drums his fingers on the laptop, like there's something he's waiting for me to understand. Finally he sighs and opens a drawer, removing a manila file and passing it across the desk.

I read the report inside. It's obvious Rich has contributed nothing to it because it's exactly what I want. He must have delegated it to the research department.

"See? Sometimes it's a banana, but sometimes it's other stuff. And it doesn't just go on her nose. There are all these clips on here of her starting on one guy, and then he talks her into putting on the blindfold, and guess what? He switches places with his friend. And then they'll bring back the banana. The point is—"

I tune him out. The summary of Gringo's organizational structure says managers kick four percent of their net gross to the corporate office, as well as three percent for marketing. If there was some kind of franchising agreement I could see how Frank might be allowed to take money from the register, but there's nothing in the report to suggest that's the case.

Frank is stealing.

"Rich. From what I'm reading here Frank isn't just hurting his employees. He's hurting his employers. We can make the case that Ferndekamp's system is bad for everyone. And if we apply that template to constituents and taxpayers . . . "

Rich looks back at his screen and squints. "Huh," he says. "Yeah."

"Hello? Rich? Frank is stealing from Gringo's. This makes Ferndekamp look like an asshole in like six different ways."

Rich looks up at me, his eyelids low, then goes back to typing. I remind myself to e-mail Ann about the transcription problem since Rich will obviously be worthless.

"If Frank is ripping off Gringo's," I say, "it adds a whole new layer to the story. He isn't just mistreating employees."

Rich spins the laptop around again. The blonde girl with the banana is on another site now, still blindfolded but now dressed as a cheerleader.

"See?" Rich says. "Slight twist, but basically the same scenario. She goes to this costume party, but her boyfriend and his dad trade costumes—"

"Hey. Rich. We have porn in Arizona, too. Can we talk about something real for two seconds?"

He turns the screen back toward himself.

"Wouldn't you consider it a big deal," I say, "if this manager wasn't just fucking around with employees but also ripping off stockholders? Not in a big way, of course, but maybe they have some totally inadequate form of oversight that allows this to happen at other Gringo's, too. And that's a good thing to know about a company, right?"

His eyes go back to the screen.

"What I'm saying, Rich, is that if someone wants to be secretary of labor, he should manage his own restaurants better than this. He's not just letting his employee be abused. He's letting his stockholders get screwed. For all we know every Gringo's has someone stealing. This could be systemic."

He pushes the laptop to the side and rocks in the chair. I appreciate his pretending to consider what I've said but I've seen this move before.

"Scott," he says, "one reason this president is in office is that people don't want the government telling them what to do. If they wanted someone lecturing them all the time they would have voted for the other guy."

He looks down at the polar bear.

"The average person doesn't care if some regular Joe takes a few bucks from the cash register," he says. "The average person wants a story. A simple narrative with a good guy and a bad guy. And a victim. Preferably a girl."

I glance over at the laptop. The picture on the screen is the cheerleader, still blindfolded, blowing various dudes. Of course she's on a hotel comforter.

"I know," Rich says. "You're appalled. Why does it have to be a girl in trouble? Isn't that sexist? And yes, it is. But we have to follow basic storytelling conventions. If people wanted their news complicated, the lead story every night would be, what, Africa or something."

I can feel him getting ready to repeat all his pat arguments: TV is a visual, personality-driven medium. There's a place for complicated, nuanced stories, but that place is in the inside sections of newspapers. The conglomerate that owns our network has sold all its newspapers. So we tell stories regular people understand.

"Rich, this story isn't that complicated."

"Really?" He puts his hands behind his head and leans back. "Pitch it to me."

"What? I just did. You were looking at blindfolded cheerleader incest."

"That wasn't a pitch," he says. "A pitch is this: blindfolded chick sucks the wrong dick. Excuse me, sucks the wrong penis. Since you're so easily offended."

"Dick is fine."

"Great," he says. "Now you're talking like a human."

He reaches into a desk and pulls out a cigar, putting it in his mouth without lighting it. "Have you read any of those things I've forwarded you from the Poynter Institute?" He puts his hands on his desk. "Because they've put more thought into news than probably either of us have. And what they say is that we can deliver reports or tell stories. Which one do you want to do?"

I nod to show I'm not arguing with the Poynter Institute. Even though I can't imagine anyone there agreeing with him.

"My source is telling us about workplace violations," Rich says. "That's our narrative. This guy who wants to be the secretary of labor— who wants to be in charge of preventing workplace violations—owns restaurants that are full of them. Boom. That's the story. Boom. Now you just need to find the violations. I mean, uncover them."

He leans back again and puts his feet on the desk. At some point he's slid them back into his loafers. It feels like a compromise.

"This stealing from the register thing? It just throws things off," he says. "It confuses the whole pitch. I'm pitching blindfolded chick sucks wrong dick. You're pitching blindfolded chick sucks wrong dick, but then we find out the guy getting sucked off is embezzling from the guy who runs the porn site, and which one's the real victim, and it's not the guy or even the guys doing her wrong but it's the *system*, man, we're all victims of the system."

He puts his feet back on the floor and leans across his desk.

"And by the way, what happened to that thing with the guys jerking off in tacos or whatever it was? The guys with the song? *That's* a fucking story."

"Look," I say, "I'm with you. We have to tell a story. Of course. But how can we know at this point what the story is? What if part of the story is that Ferndekamp is more incompetent than evil?"

He looks at me like I must be misunderstanding.

"Scott," he says, "let's not give people more than they can handle. We can learn a lot from porn. This is what people want at their most basic level. Take something incredibly simple—in this case sex, but it could be anything—and make it totally, completely understandable. Give it to the people."

He plays another drum roll on his laptop, looking me in the eye. I break the gaze by shaking my head and he starts typing again. He spins the computer so the screen is facing me.

"So the girl goes to get an abortion," he says. "But while she's sedated, this doctor, Dr. Fuchslutz—"

"Jesus," I say. "How do you get off on this stuff? The whole tricking women routine?"

He shrugs, double-clicks the mouse.

"I didn't have any sisters," he says, tilting his head thoughtfully. "That probably doesn't help."

TEMPE, Ariz., Feb. 9 Every day I follow Keegan down the useless planks of former train tracks, through the dried-up streams of former Indian villages being turned into condos. She's training for a marathon. Today's trail leads past an abandoned mine up a ridge to the top of a mountain where the view is supposed to be ancient and beautiful. I try to keep up.

"So, hey," I call up to her. "Are we still worried about Carlotta Espinoza?"

She keeps her eyes on the trail. "Ann and Hanlon have a secret plan for if she tries to talk," she says through measured breaths. "Something brutal."

The breeze picks up, warm and acidic. At least there's no mud. It hasn't rained here in months.

"Brutal like stabbing her in the neck? Brutal how?"

"Brutal I can't say how."

"You can't say because you can't tell me or can't say because you don't know?"

She moves skillfully over burrs and stones, her efficiency contributing as much to the space between us as her speed.

"Because I don't know."

She sounds embarrassed, even through the filter of muggy air between us. I'm giddy at the thought that we're equally uninformed, then embarrassed that I care.

"What about Ferndekamp? Any idea on a timeline? On a confirmation hearing?"

"I feel like we keep having this conversation," she calls back to me. "A split Senate isn't gonna, like, ram through the president's first choice. This isn't the most popular administration."

I try to make out the words over the sound of our feet.

"You don't have to be, like, cranky," I call out. "If you aren't worried, great."

"Of course I'm worried," she yells. "It's my job. You just have to report."

She glances back to see if I'm going to argue, her ponytail whipping as she turns. I lower my eyes to the ground.

"We've got a few more weeks, at least," she says. "We'll be fine, as long as we get back on course."

Her voice is more quiet, almost gentle, like this is a subject she hadn't wanted to raise.

"Back on course?"

She digs in. Chunks of rock break off at her feet and I space my steps to keep from slipping. Finally we get to the top and the sky seems to open up around us, vast and empty.

We pull ourselves up into a tall wooden bench looking out over the valley. The desert brown is interrupted by honeycombs of development and swatches of chemical green. The unnaturally dark blues are swimming pools and manmade lakes.

Keegan tugs at her shoelace.

"You said 'back on course,'" I say. "Do you think I'm fucking this up?"

She takes off her shoe and adjusts the sock, looking down at the dirt. Black ants carry something the color of molasses.

"Ann was pretty pissed we lost all that time getting your glasses fixed," she says.

I lean back so my feet won't swing from the bench. "How was that my fault?"

"Look, I don't want to fight about this," she says. "I'm just asking you to be really careful."

Her voice is more like a girlfriend's than a supervisor's. I tell myself to recognize an offering and to please not say anything stupid.

"I will. Of course."

She shakes out her shoe. "Thank you."

We've both seen reporters seize control from producers by withholding information. She's not just thanking me for agreeing to be careful but for not challenging her. She puts her shoe on and I look at the dust on her cheeks. I wish I could tell her about Christmas Eve. I wonder if all the withholding now will make it harder to be honest when she isn't my boss anymore.

"Hey," I say. "Can I kiss you?"

She bites her lip like she's happy I asked but doesn't want me to know. It's not a yes but I treat it like one and reach up to hold her face in my hands. I smudge the dust with one thumb and press down on her mouth with the other. She smiles, more shy than I was expecting. I move my right hand to the back of her neck and my left hand to the top of her thigh, digging my thumb into the soft skin, moving my hand inside her shorts. She reaches down to stop my hand on her thigh and I laugh and kiss her neck until she relents enough for me to grip the elastic and cotton of her waistband to tug her closer. She slaps my arm, annoyed or playful I don't know. I kiss her mouth and try to maneuver our heads so that if her eyes are open she'll see the sky and maybe think of what she's seeing now when she thinks of me.

I'm thinking about what to write with my tongue, but the taste of salt and dust in Keegan's mouth suddenly gives me writer's block.

She tastes like Harper used to after hikes.

I force myself to picture Harper's face to see if I can do it objectively, imagining one feature at a time, but when I get to her eyes it hurts too much and I have to stop.

Keegan notices something's wrong.

"Hey." She wrenches away. "I'm not . . . feeling this."

She jumps down to the dirt, straightening her shorts, then ties her shoe and starts to run. I follow her slowly, back to her Tomahawk, and watch her pat around the top of the right front tire for the key she's stashed there. I feel like I should come up with something to tell her, something supportive but not annoyingly apologetic.

"Hey," I say. "Have I told you Frank has a security system?"

TEMPE, Ariz., Feb. 10 Today's forwarded mail includes three envelopes addressed to Harper from the City of Los Angeles. When I accidentally/on purpose open them it turns out she has three unpaid parking tickets for parking her Honda Civic on the same stretch of San Fernando Road. I try to guess why she keeps going there—some new guy?—and then realize exactly who she's been seeing.

Benjamin.

Benjamin—pronounced ben-ha-meen—is this gay Salvadorean kid one of her friends in the sociology department wanted us to mentor. He was living in a bad part of Highland Park and gangbangers would kick his ass every day because he'd been openly gay since eighth grade. When we met him, he was a sophomore and wanted to be a journalist. Harper's friend thought we could help him.

This was about a year ago, when Harper was done with the stripping part of her thesis and was working on the writing. I would stay up with her every night helping her sort through interviews with dancers from the 1940s or reading her drafts. She never had time to write during the day because she was volunteering for so many on-campus causes. Meanwhile we were trying to be vegans, which meant we made dinner at home almost every night before going for hikes at Runyon Canyon. All the cooking and hiking and reading left me with maybe five hours a night to sleep so I was drinking two or three Diet Cokes a day to stay functional at work.

At Runyon we hiked up the trails to the hills. She would tell me about her day and try to get me to volunteer for one cause or another and I would say my heart was in it but I just couldn't.

"Why not?" she would ask.

"Because I work for the news. We're supposed to be unbiased."

"So you can't sign a petition asking the city to use more renewable energy? Who's against renewable energy?"

"I don't know. Oil companies. I don't want to be doing a story on new hybrid vehicles and have some oil company say I'm biased."

"But you are biased. You drive a Prius."

"Right, but that's a personal decision. I could say it's just for the cheap gas and there's nothing political involved. Signing something is advocacy. Network policies specifically ban advocacy. You can believe whatever you want, but you can't advocate for it."

There was a lookout we liked at the top of the hills. We always got to it as the coyotes started crying. I'm pretty sure they shrieked through every one of these talks.

"What about freedom of speech?"

"I know, it's ridiculous. But you lose some of your freedom of speech when you join the press. I don't want to discredit my own report by signing a petition."

"How would anyone know?"

"I don't know. Don't petitions stay on file somewhere?"

Howling, crying, the sun going down. Owners scooping up their dogs in case the coyotes were calling out positions.

"What if the people on one side of an issue are totally wrong?"

"They might think you're totally wrong. You act like their opinions are as valid as anyone else's and let viewers sort it out."

"You can't *help* them sort it out?"

Of course we tried to help sort it out. When people said things that weren't true we always tried to point it out. But how often do you catch someone in a flat-out lie?

"Harp, we have to report for the whole country, not just smoking-hot graduate students at UCLA."

Runyon doesn't have crickets. But if it did.

At some point she started throwing causes at me just to see how far I would take the neutrality thing. Was it okay to vote? Sure, I said. Voting was private.

"Okay," she said. "Can you tell *other* people how to vote? Because, you know. In your job you always know about those propositions no one understands."

Flattery. I asked how many people.

"Your girlfriend," she said.

"Sure."

"Her parents."

"Her parents live in Virginia. I don't know how much help I would be."

"People you meet at a party."

"How well do I know them?"

"You don't. But your girlfriend says they're cool. She promises they won't tell anyone you helped them."

"Are you making fun of me?"

"So people at parties—doubtful."

She always talked about what she wanted in terms of what she wanted to change.

Benjamin was one of the few causes I couldn't think of any reason not to get involved in. Whatever I told him would be career advice. If meeting with us after school happened to keep him indoors during the hours he would normally be getting his ass kicked, so much the better. We met at a donut place on San Fernando Road because it was close to his bus stop. Of course there was never any parking.

Harper drank coffee and I drank Diet Coke and Benjamin ate donuts we bought him. He told us the first article he wanted to write was about how God had made him gay, he hadn't had a choice, and how people who called him names or beat him up were doing the same thing to God, because God had made him in His own image.

Harper told him he needed to apply to college if he wanted to be a journalist and that college would get him away from the neighborhood idiots who kept attacking him. She said we could help him find scholarships and that his article would also make an awesome admissions essay. She and I could help him polish it up so it would be as good on paper as it was when he explained it. She looked at me like it was my turn to say something smart and encouraging.

Benjamin looked like an intelligent kid. He wore a Smiths T-shirt and wire-rimmed glasses, but seemed to be playing with the clichés of high-school homosexuality. A thin mustache and broad shoulders gave him a look of confidence that transcended the passive stereotype. I decided not to bullshit him.

"Everything Harper is saying is exactly right," I said. "But the thing is, being a reporter isn't about saying what you think is right. You actually lose the right to say what you think is right. You have to report what other people say, a lot of the time, even if you think it's wrong."

His narrowed his eyes like he was trying to understand what I really meant, as if the overt message was too obvious.

"Right," he said. "But aren't there different kinds of stories? Like with Hurricane Katrina, when all those reporters pretty much said flat-out that the government messed up—"

Harper nodded quickly, a signal for me to get back to the hopeful stuff. I looked at Benjamin.

"Well . . . okay," I said. "But you can't really take a stand like that and have people believe you if you're taking stands all the time."

Harper picked up a pen, acted like she was taking notes. "And can you tell us exactly how often it's okay for reporters to tell the truth, as opposed to being neutral?"

I blinked at her. It was kind of cute, the thing with the pen.

"Like, if I was doing a story on gay marriage, which would probably never happen because most of my stories are about fake trends and dead starlets, I couldn't just say at the end, 'By the way, in my opinion gay marriage is a matter of equal protection under the law for all people regardless of sexual orientation.'"

Benjamin shrugged. "Because the facts have to speak for themselves."

Harper put down her pen. She looked at him approvingly, then at me: See? He gets it.

But I wasn't sure he did.

"But there's still the problem," I said, "that what you consider facts might not be facts to someone else."

Harper nodded exaggeratedly—please, *we get it*—then turned to Benjamin.

"So basically," she said, "to keep your credibility you have to ignore things that are totally credible."

Benjamin laughed. I made a face. She was going to lock him into her philosophy before I could even articulate mine.

"Yeah," I said. "Not exactly. What I'm really trying to say is that reporters are more like moderators than debaters. If you're pushing for one side, you might want to think about whether to be a reporter. You might want to be an activist, like Harper."

I wanted to make sure the kid understood his options. He turned to Harper.

"What kind of activist are you?" he asked.

I answered before she could.

"She's involved in all kinds of causes at UCLA. Divesting from Sudan, animal rights, protecting the ocean—like last week, she was circulating this petition about warning labels for pregnant women so they wouldn't eat tuna. But I couldn't sign it because I might have to do a story about it someday."

"It was about mercury poisoning," Harper cut in. "Scott didn't want to seem anti-poison. Or pro-baby."

I ignored the dig.

"One of the nice things about being a reporter is that some of the time people believe you," I said. "If you're always giving opinions people think you're crying wolf. Which is why a lot of people unfortunately don't listen to activists."

Harper shook her head, eyeing me: Fine, you got your licks in. Can we get back to helping the kid? Benjamin took his bus schedule from his backpack and started stacking his sugary napkins like we would all be leaving soon.

"I guess," he said. "Maybe. But people are kind of . . . stupid sometimes. What do you do if one side is obviously right?"

Maybe he would make a good reporter. He already knew the trick about asking your most incendiary question last.

"Well, that's the thing," I said. "Can you name a single issue where one side is obviously right?"

"Darfur," Harper said.

"Gay marriage," Benjamin said. "Gay rights."

"Mercury," she added. "Warning pregnant women not to eat mercury."

Benjamin looked at her and she beamed back. There was no stopping them now.

"The Civil Rights movement."

"World War II."

"Slavery."

"Apartheid."

"Okay," I said. "Okay. But take civil rights. If reporters had gone on the news every single night and said, 'Jim Crow laws are wrong, public places should be integrated,' would the right side have won? Or would middle America have tuned out the news and said, 'Forget it, these people are telling me how to think, I'm not listening?'"

Benjamin stared into his pile of napkins, considering. Harper took a sip of coffee.

"What really got the average American to realize the Civil Rights movement was right was seeing all these racist cops turning hoses and dogs on people who weren't doing anything except demonstrating, peacefully. The news presented the images, showed people the facts of what was happening, and regular people figured out for themselves who was on the right side."

Harper broke out laughing. It felt a little stagey.

"Are you seriously saying," she said, "that reporters were the big heroes of the Civil Rights movement? Because I thought it was Martin Luther King, and Coretta Scott King, and Rosa Parks, and all the other *activists* who actually did things as opposed to the people who took their pictures."

Benjamin tried not to laugh but couldn't help it. He looked at me to see if I would laugh too: I had to concede now, right? To my girlfriend?

When we went outside there was a parking ticket on my windshield.

"No good deed goes unpunished," I said, lifting the ticket to show Harper.

"That's retarded," she said.

My face felt hot. The whole argument had seemed unfair. I couldn't bring up one of the biggest, most obvious reasons to stay neutral, the reason that might mean the most to a kid trying to get out of a poor neighborhood. I brought it up the next morning.

"I don't want to make a huge issue of this," I said. "But how much do you think Benjamin would get paid to be an activist?"

She was putting on earrings in the medicine cabinet mirror. She didn't look for my reflection.

"I don't know," she said. "You're the one who wants him to be an activist."

I opened the medicine cabinet, looking for toothpaste, trying to make her look at me.

"I just mean if he wants to take stands on issues, which is great, he should be an activist," I said. "But I'm worried that he wouldn't be able to move away unless he has kind of a higher paying job."

I closed the mirror. She was still staring straight ahead.

"I know," she said. "Reporter."

I brushed my teeth, not saying anything. She walked out of the bathroom, to the bedroom closet, and started reconsidering her shoes.

"My point is, if he wants to be a reporter for a major network, for example, or a newspaper, he's gonna have to kind of follow the party line on being fair and neutral. I just don't want to give him false hope that he can just charge in and start changing the world."

She stepped into a pair of pair of synthetic-leather heels, looked herself over in the full-length mirror. I stared at her reflection and lost my train of thought.

"Well, of course," she said. "What I'm hoping is that once he gets pretty well-established at his network, or newspaper, he might try to work from the inside to make things better, and not just complain about what dumb stories he has to do."

I leaned into the wall, crossing my arms.

"That's probably easier to say if you have really rich parents," I said.

She kicked off the shoes. "Don't talk about my parents," she said. "Your parents are lawyers from the Berkeley Hills."

"Are we still talking about Benjamin?"

She glared at me in the mirror.

"It's kind of hard to figure out what you want when you say you agree with what I'm doing, and you hate what you're doing, but you keep doing it anyway. If you're doing it for the money, don't."

She sat on the bed, pulled on sneakers. She took out her earrings and tossed them on the nightstand.

"Is it possible," I said, "that I could do it for the money and because I think it's the right thing to do?"

"I wouldn't press it all the time if you did."

A few months after that, in August, she came home one night and said some of her friends had invited her to come to Virginia to help save the state from some lunatic on the wrong side of every issue we had ever cared about. She asked if I wanted to come with her.

She said this could be our chance to make a difference on something that really mattered, and we could do it together. Her thesis was practically finished; she could be done in a week. She felt like there was no way she couldn't go.

I was so caught up in the trial at this point I was drinking four Diet Cokes a day and had given up completely on trying to be vegan. I said something about "career suicide" and that there was no way I could go. We went back and forth about whether she had to be gone for so long—another fight that didn't seem so important at the time—and then she left. After she was gone I offered to help in secret ways—to tell her how to dumb down press releases so the local media would understand them—but she said her side wanted to win without dumbing things down. When the election was over she came back and then left me for good.

I look at the dates on Harper's parking tickets and see that they're all from the time between the start of the trial and when she left for Virginia. It hadn't occurred to me that she might keep meeting Benjamin by herself. She stopped thinking of us as connected long before I did.

I wonder if she still sees him and if she says anything about me if she does. I find my checkbook and pay the tickets so they won't discourage her from all the good she's doing, somewhere, wherever she is.

TEMPE, Ariz., Feb. 14 When I mop I imagine that the chemicals in the Lim Lam are so strong they're turning the air around me into vaporized scotch and within a few minutes I feel stoned whether I am or not. Sometimes there's a moment when I wonder if the high comes from solvent at all or if I might be genuinely enjoying myself at the job I'm pretending to do, the way Harper started to like stripping. I don't miss having to deal with deadlines and meetings, and I like that no one has a computer here except Frank. The best part is that I'm not allowed to use my cell phone except during breaks.

I'm almost done mopping the men's room when a fat guy in a dirty Cardinals cap comes in to claim a stall, sitting down with an involuntary-sounding noise. I put my mop in its bucket and head out the door.

The STAC pamphlet says male customers should be left alone in the bathroom for no more than five minutes. Women get twelve. When time is up an employee is supposed to find some excuse to enter the bathroom and make sure the customer isn't tagging, sleeping, or committing suicide. Five free minutes gives me time to check in with Maria.

Ann's given me permission to try to feel Maria out about how to get access to Frank's videotapes. I want to know what he might be catching on his cameras that I might be missing on mine. I find Maria at the register and ask what's going on. She looks at me and shakes her head.

"Nothing," she says.

She sounds like I used to when part of my job at the network was monitoring reports from other news agencies. Some jaded senior producer would ask me what was happening in the world and I would read the day's incoming stories: 78 percent of American children say their dream job is "celebrity." Michael Jackson wishes to clear up several rumors. The author of the glue-addiction memoir *Stuck* is sniffing again. "Nothing," I would say.

Maria hasn't left me any opening, but my Lim Lam high gives me the confidence to press on.

"So," I say. "Just wondering. Is Frank the only one who opens up in the morning, or does someone else have a key, like, just in case?"

She reaches into her pocket and slaps a key on the counter.

"Nice," I say. "Anyone else?"

She slumps her shoulders and looks straight ahead at nothing.

"Julio," she says.

I wonder what he's done to impress Frank in such a short time.

"Anyone else?"

"Juan," she says. "And Carlos. Bethany. Really everyone. You don't have one?"

I shake my head. It doesn't seem fair that I'm the sole exception to the key policy. I've messed up, sure, but I haven't given him any reason to doubt my honesty. How am I supposed to steal his tapes without a key?

"Maybe it's because Frank thinks you're on drugs," Maria says. "I told him you're not. You argue too much."

"Thanks," I say, trying not to look high.

"Sure."

"Why did he hire me," I ask, "if he thought I was on drugs?"

She looks at me with eyes full of well-informed pity.

"He likes giving people a second chance. Bethany used to be on drugs. Now she's into Jesus. It's just how Frank is."

I want to ask what drugs Bethany was on but a squawk comes from the drive-thru booth, announcing a new customer pulling up to the sign.

"I'll handle it," I say. I try to sound decisive, responsible. Sober.

As I put on the headset I hear the operator say, "Ah, yes. Aha, yes. Yes, aha. No black in coffee. No sir. No black." The voice is obsequious, meek.

"Maria," I say, "what happened to the Jamaicans?"

She looks bored. "They're in Thailand now."

My heart drops.

"The . . . Jamaicans are in Thailand?"

She exhales, annoyed. "The entire call center is in Thailand. They fired the Jamaicans. They started talking about unionizing and asking for raises and benefits."

"Um," I say. "Wow."

The driver pulls up to the window, already glaring at me. He's around forty, balding, slightly heavyset.

And Asian.

"Hey," he says. "Next time you decide to pull the Charlie Chan routine through the speaker, try to remember that none of us can tell Rs from Ls. And make some clever jokes about all of us taking pictures and singing karaoke and driving badly and—you know what? Forget it. Just let me talk to your manager."

Frank gives me the lecture in his office this time. I take mental notes on everything—any cameras trained on the women's bathroom? Any piles of money lying around?—in case this is the last time I'm here. I'll be lucky to keep my job.

"Why were you even in the booth?" he says. "No, don't answer. Why weren't you in the bathroom, cleaning? Wait, no. I don't want to know."

I do mental calculation as he talks. I make about $85,000 a year at the network. I don't know how to do anything else.

"Are you trying to make me fire you? Do you not like it here? Are you too smart for us? If you are, why can't you figure out how to stay at your station?"

Losing my fake job, and my real one as a result, would be a relief at first. Then depressing. I imagine myself moving into a studio apartment, or my parents' house, just to save while I figured things out. Then I imagine never figuring things out.

I don't want a job that requires me to crush other people for money, but I couldn't live as well as I do working one of the jobs of the guiltless.

"Why are you here, really? Because you obviously don't care. Is it amusing to you? Is it funny? Do you like the idea that everyone is working hard except you?"

Frank stops and looks past me to the door. It's Maria. She looks sick.

"The men's room is totally flooded, filled with sludge," she says. "Some guy was in there for like twenty minutes."

I turn to Frank. He covers his face with his hands.

"So," Maria says, "I guess . . . I'll fix it?"

"No," I say. "I'll do it."

Neither of them objects. I walk out of the office and down the hall, past the counter and down the other hall to the bathroom. I open the door and squint at black deposits coagulating in the corners of the uneven floor, buckled low enough to keep the blackness from seeping out to the hall. Silty liquid laps the hem of my $180 jeans—money well spent—as I drag the bucket of Lim Lam inside. The wheels swish through muck. I dip my hand into the bucket and wipe Lim Lam under my nose like they do with VapoRub in police procedurals, just before they open a body bag.

Maria makes an "Out of Order" sign and runs a line of tape from the hall to the left side of the front doors, giving me a clear path to carry buckets of sludge to the Dumpsters. I go through the heads of five mops and Maria runs out to the grocery store to get me more, along with a tall bottle of water I'm pretty sure she pays for herself. I almost hug her.

After two hours Frank leans in the door, probably to fire me, but when he sees the black water he just turns and goes back to his office. The time for the network teleconference comes and goes, along with the time for my shift to end, and when Julio comes in for his shift he pokes his head into the men's room and immediately runs out to the parking lot to puke.

At about three o'clock Frank grants Maria permission to call home and ask her mom if she can watch Olivia for a few extra hours because of a work emergency. She comes in to help me mop, working twice as fast as I do, and I feel as embarrassed as I would be if I'd made the mess myself, which I kind of did. We work almost silently, pointing each other toward bits of wet toilet paper or clumps of black hair behind the toilets. The only break I take is to text Keegan that I'm sorry I missed the teleconference and that I won't be back until late, which works out well because I'm not sure what people do for Valentine's Day when they're just fucking.

By the time it's dark I've convinced Maria that things will go faster if she dabs some Lim Lam under her nostrils, and before long we aren't dabbing anymore but slapping it undiluted over our lips and down our chins. While we mop we make jokes about going brain-dead from the chemicals, and I say it's a good thing she's already had a kid and she says "ewwww" and punches me in the arm, laughing. By now I'm so high it feels like an invitation so I punch her back, harder than she expects. She pinches me and I slap the backs of her arms and she says if I don't stop she'll never teach me the greatest trick in the history of fast food: how to put lids on drinks so they pop off as soon as customers leave the drive-thru.

When Frank deems the men's room clean enough to enter he comes in and looks around, poking his head under the sink and studying the ceiling as if we might have missed some stray fecal matter dangling over our heads. As he walks out he says, "See you two tomorrow."

I'm not fired.

Maria throws down her mop and gives me a hug I'm sure Keegan will ask me about but I don't care. It's been so long since I've felt this feeling that I need a few seconds to recognize it as pride.

TEMPE, Ariz., Feb. 15 In drug movies the hero narc has to do heroin to keep his cover. In mob movies the undercover fed has to shoot someone. In terrorism movies he has to plant bombs, then pray he can tell his superiors where they're hidden before it's too late.

I have to eat carne asada.

Frank slides the paper plate across our table at Filiberto's, a place two blocks from Gringo's. He brings me here after saying we should have lunch today—"somewhere good"—so we walk a few blocks to a restaurant located in the parking lot of a shopping center with a Planned Parenthood and bartending school and tattoo parlor. The plastic surface of our table is hot from the sun and Frank says Filiberto's carne asada is the best he's ever had, anywhere. He ordered it for both of us.

Staying late to clean the bathroom turns out to be the best career move I've ever made, both at the network and Gringo's. Ann and Rich are thrilled that I've caught Frank in so many "workplace violations": coerced overtime, unsanitary working conditions, hostile work environment. Never mind that none of it would have happened if I'd followed the five-minute rule.

Frank bites into a piece of meat and his face fills with more satisfaction that anyone should get from food. The meat is piled onto a corn tostada I ordinarily wouldn't eat because of the carbs, but now the tostada and beans seem like my only friends. I haven't eaten red meat since ninth grade, when my mom took me to Carl's Jr. to show us it wasn't worth it.

"They don't weigh out the meat here before they serve it," Frank says. "It must cost them a ton, but Jesus, is it good. At Gringo's, you got corporate keeping track of every ounce—you'll see. Someday."

He takes another bite and I think about slaughterhouses, cows force-fed wheat instead of grass, abscesses growing in their stomachs, cows still awake as they're attached to hooks and whisked upside-down over the killing floor.

Frank gnashes the meat in his mouth, grinding it from side to side. He looks like a cow. Or a bull. He swallows.

"You saying grace or something? Eat up."

I shake my head, try to pick out the smallest chunk of steak on the plate. The mention of grace makes me wish I knew when Lent was. I could say I'd given up meat for it. I'm not worried that refusing to eat will offend him. I'm worried about him being embarrassed. There's no tactful way to say no to something that brings someone else so much satisfaction.

I fork a piece of meat and put it in my mouth, leaving it on my tongue long enough for the reality to set in: I'm eating meat. I start to chew, and it's a totally different sensation than I was expecting. Instead of being soft and fatty the meat is elastic, strong, with just the right amount of give. Each bite is a close contest I know I'll win. I thought the meat would taste like soy slathered in butter, but it feels more alive than that: wet and grisly and aware.

"See?" Frank says. I take another bite, mixing in some guacamole this time. So this is how people get fat. I think of Kanye West rapping about something so wrong feeling so right but remember that song is about diamonds and take another bite to forget.

Frank puts his fork down and wipes his fingers on a napkin before re-engaging his food. I copy him, trying to score points. People never bond over big ideas, just steak and football. This is probably why I have so few male friends.

"So," Frank says. "Looks like Maria's got a little thing for you."

My face feels hot. This is the scene in the drug movie where the bad guy is about to tell the narc something important but the narc is too high to understand. At least I'm wearing the glasses. All I have to do is keep him talking.

"Really?"

"Doesn't it seem like it?" He puts down his carne asada, half-wraps it in foil to take a break. He takes his first sip of Coke, regular Coke, the same kind he ordered for me.

"I don't know." I take the smallest sip possible. Eating meat is one thing but I'm not going to start with regular Coke, too.

"She helped you clean the bathroom, didn't she?"

"Well, yeah, but . . . wasn't that for overtime?"

He reopens his foil, wags a finger as if to chide me for trying to trick him. "I'd love to give you overtime," he says. "But."

He holds his hands out over the carne asada and shrugs: This is all he can offer. I picture Ann, her eyes moist and hands clapped together: *He paid you in meat.*

"Oh, no," I say, "of course not for me. No way. I just meant for her."

I take another bite and say, "Mmm," like the meat is my real focus, the conversation an afterthought. Just keep him talking. He pushes his plate a few inches away and pats his stomach.

"Maria's more . . . complicated," he says. "But is her thing for you maybe mutual?"

This doesn't feel like a question a boss should ask but it doesn't feel illegal either.

"I've never thought about it." I look across the parking lot at two girls coming out of Planned Parenthood and going into the bartending school. "She's really young."

"She is," Frank says. "She sure is."

He pulls his plate back toward him, picks up the tostado for a big bite.

"Eighteen," he says. "I remember being eighteen. She's a lot more mature than I was."

"She's actually nineteen."

Frank looks up, surprised. "Right," he says. "Sorry."

I wrap up my asada, wondering if I can get away with not eating anymore. I don't want to get hooked.

"So you do like her."

I pretend to be distracted by the girls coming out of the bartending school, going back into Planned Parenthood. I try to look like someone with all the options in the world. "I don't know," I say. "I guess you get mature faster if you have a kid."

Frank sips his Coke. "Oh, definitely. I didn't have a kid until I was 32."

He gives me a look that seems approving: it's smart of me not to have kids. "But she was mature even before," he says. "She should be in college."

"Yeah."

"If you do like her," Frank says, lowering his voice, "maybe you can put a bug in her ear. Be a good influence. You're a smart guy. That's probably why she likes you."

"Thanks."

I finally get why he's brought me here. When someone strikes me as not-quite impossibly stupid I always compliment their intelligence, almost to shame them into being smart. Frank's pulling the same routine on me, throwing in Maria as an added motivation.

"Maybe you would want to . . . take classes together," he says. "Management, hospitality. Like that. Corporate smiles on that."

He leans back, taking in the view of the parking lot.

"Of course," he says, "you'd have to stop with the arguing."

I smile. None of this is personal to him. Everything is a management technique. I don't know if the network doesn't bother with mind games or if I'm too brainwashed to notice them anymore.

I pick up a napkin and blow my nose. I was hoping Frank would say something out-of-bounds about Maria but he's turned things around so it looks like I'm the one who might be chasing around a nineteen-year-old. It's almost like he knows this could end up on television.

I want the focus back on him.

"So I don't know if it's my place to ask this."

Frank wraps his remaining scraps of tostada into a foil ball and wipes a napkin over his side of the table before he looks at me. "Fire away."

"Again, sorry if this is . . . I'm not sure how to say this. But with Juan and Carlos, you know how they're always singing that song?"

He tilts his head, his face a blank. I should have asked better, in a complete sentence. Now we'll have to clean things up with a voiceover.

"What I mean is, Juan and Carlos have been singing a song about . . . violating cleanliness standards, right? And I was just thinking, if they're actually doing that stuff, wouldn't that be—you know, pretty far off from the STAC system?"

He looks at me and then the table, wringing his hands like he's working up to a confession. He looks at me again, like I might help him, and finally answers.

"I'm sorry," he says. "I don't know what you mean."

He sounds surprisingly convincing.

"Come on, Frank. You know the song. The thing about . . . bodily fluids ending up in the food."

He bats his ball of foil from side-to-side like a cat, like he can ignore me into relenting. But he can't.

"I'm talking about semen, Frank."

He looks at me with raised eyebrows and I stare back. Finally he gets up and dumps his plate in the trash, then sits down and leans across the table.

"How long were you mopping this morning?" he says. "I know sometimes, when the Lim Lam isn't properly diluted—"

I start singing the song in Spanish, phonetically, stopping after each line to translate. He finally recognizes the tune and stops me before I get to the part about tomatoes.

"Scott," he says, "your Spanish is terrible."

I lean back, adjusting the fanny pack in my lap. Frank laughs.

I have the lyrics completely wrong.

The song, he says, is a huge hit on Spanish radio. It's by a reggaeton artist named Grande Boca. Frank asks if I know what that means and I say Big Mouth. He seems surprised that I know. He says I have the melody right, more or less, but that the lyrics have nothing to do with food. They're about Grande Boca going to a party filled with too many beautiful women. No one ejaculates on anything.

"At least," Frank says, "not during the song. Maybe after."

I remember thinking it was weird that the transcription people didn't make any typos. I throw away my trash and we walk back to Gringo's. I wish I could explain to Frank that it wasn't my fault, that we have a team of transcribers in charge of translating everything for us, except in this case they weren't translating at all. They made the whole thing up, just to throw off our investigation.

The Evil Empire is at it again.

SCOTTSDALE, Ariz., Feb. 18 Maria says I'm invited to Olivia's birthday party. It's a huge coup. I try to think of reasons she might want me there but I keep coming back to believing she actually enjoys my company.

Ann authorizes Keegan and me to spend fifteen dollars on a present and we go to the mall. As we pull into the parking lot at Scottsdale Fashion Square, I'm already imagining my on-camera interview with Maria. Before the report is ready to air—when we've got enough to run with, but still have time to add a surprise guest—I'll show up at her house and tell her we'll fly her and her mom and Olivia to New York, first-class. We'll put them up somewhere good and we'll send her mom and Olivia to the park to play so Maria and I can go over the questions I'll have carefully fashioned to make sure she comes off looking good.

Yes, she'll say. She took the money. The admission will give her instant credibility. She'll say she only accepted it because she was scared of losing her job. It was all Frank's idea. At some point I'll have to ask if he did anything to her.

She might say yes. I'll say I'm so furious at Frank that I don't care about the broadcast, that I'm going to fly back to Arizona and crack his teeth. She'll shake her head like she understands tragedy in a way I never will and say I can't sink to his level, that she can't do the broadcast without my help. We'll do the interview for real, on the air. By the end of the show every other news agency in the country will try to book her but she'll turn them all down. I'll take her out for a drink, some place near NYU where they don't card, and if they do I'll take a break from all my dietary rules and buy her an ice cream, and not make a move on her, no matter what, unless she makes one on me first.

"What are you thinking?" Keegan says. She stops the car and hands her keys to the valet.

"Thinking?" We get out of the car and I walk after her.

"Where are you thinking we should start?"

Everything with Keegan is awkward lately and I keep trying to find excuses to touch her, just to force the issue of how casual or not casual we are. I put a hand on her back and point toward a mall directory.

There's a toy store on level three but to get to the escalators we have to walk by the art galleries on level one. Scottsdale is Arizona's answer to Beverly Hills, but with a southwestern twist that's supposed to make its displays of wealth feel less crass. The galleries are full of portraits of wolves silhouetted against purple moons and Navajos on the brink of tears at sunset and the skulls of dead cattle peering out like they're auditioning for the front of an Eagles album.

On the handful of nights Keegan and I have gone out for drinks here we've ended up at bars with indoor cacti and sculptures of forest-green Native American creatures playing lutes. Sipping our overpriced tequilas we've met guys with scary facelifts and bolo ties who give us business cards that list professions like "rancher" and "cowboy poet" and "rambler." When we press them on what they really do they mention things like foreclosures or consulting or "dabbling in the managed health game." It's hard to make some things sound folksy, even when you're a cowboy poet. We find the escalators.

Ann's e-mailed us a list of toys the Public Interest Research Group has deemed safe for one-year-olds because the last thing we want is for Olivia to choke on a button and have the network be implicated in her death. When we get to level three, none of the cool toys costs less than forty dollars, and besides that, all of them talk, so we decide to drive fifteen minutes to the Arizona Mills in Tempe. We put the top down and listen to a new song by an environmentally sensitive rapper with the chorus, "Up in a Hummer motherfuckers never see us, 'cause I'd rather catch a hummer from a vegan in a Prius."

The dashboard says it's seventy-four degrees and the day feels kind of perfect, with a clear sky and gentle sun. It's what I thought L.A. would be like before I moved there, and maybe what it is like if you live in Venice or the hills.

At the Mills people try to look richer instead of poorer and the too-young parents dragging their kids past the rainforest- and prison-themed eateries wear Old Navy jeans and T-shirts with designer's names spelled out in gold. Everything seems bigger than it has to be, from the size of the names to the signs that point out different zones of the mall in *Jurassic Park* font. Keegan and I get lost looking for the toy store and when we finally find it realize we still can't afford anything we like.

"Maybe I could just, like, make a donation in her name," I say.

Keegan takes her sunglasses out of her purse as we walk out to the parking lot.

"Wouldn't that be a little suspicious?"

"I think it would be nice."

"I don't think that many fast-food workers are making charitable donations. No offense."

"None taken. I'm not really a fast-food worker. Kind of. You know."

Last night we watched *Donnie Brasco*, where Johnny Depp is an FBI agent who goes undercover in the mob. At one point a gang war breaks out and one of the FBI guys says Depp's in danger not because he's one of us—a fed—but because he's one of them, a mobster. When he said it, Keegan looked at me and rubbed her finger under her nose like she was applying Lim Lam. It's the closest she's come to saying anything about my Valentine's Day cleanup day with Maria.

We move on to the Chandler Palladium. Chandler is like Tempe without the clean streets and good sushi and on the way we pass lettuce fields being turned into houses.

"Fifteen dollars really isn't that much," I say.

"Fifteen dollars is more than you make in like, two hours," she says. "Not *you* you, but you know."

Ann set the limit at fifteen dollars because she said it was the most she could imagine a fast food worker being able to afford on a salary of less than $200 a week. Never mind that my network apartment costs $1200 a month. Ann predicted, correctly, that no one at Gringo's would snoop around about how employees can afford to live. Gringo's doesn't want to know.

The Palladium caters to a lower-income demographic than the Fashion Square or the Mills and has a store called BearMart Express where almost every item has been approved by P.I.R.G. Keegan parks at the empty end of the parking lot and though she doesn't say it I'm sure she's thinking the same thing I am, that people with cheap cars have less reason not to bump into nice ones. When we walk through the entrance something feels off and I realize it's that the Palladium doesn't blast you with cold air as soon as you walk in like a normal mall does. On the way to BearMart we try to find things to compliment so we can pretend the mall isn't so bad.

"Oh. That pizza looks good."

"Did you . . . want some?"

"I'm just saying."

"Right. Oh, shoe store."

"Do you need shoes?"

"Yeah, actually. But not like, now."

When we get to BearMart it feels like a sad knockoff of the Build-a-Bear Workshop I've walked past in Manhattan. You choose from one of three sizes of small, naked bears made from a material that seems less cuddly than "machine-washable," then jazz them up with à la carte accessories. We seize on one of the small bears for $9.95, leaving us only $5.05 for accessories and tax. I find a medium-sized bear dressed like a princess on sale but I'm not buying Olivia a princess. I don't want her to grow up fantasizing about knights.

"Let's go," I tell Keegan. "I can't do this."

A mother drags two kids to the register and asks if they take credit cards. The saleswoman says yes, and the mother nods to her kids, a boy and a girl about four and six. They break back to the bins and pull out a pair of identical bear tuxedos. With tax they come to $21.14.

"I'll put fourteen dollars on the card," the mother says, "and the rest in cash."

The kids hand the bear outfits over the counter to be bagged. The saleswoman looks at the mother, annoyed.

"It's easier if you can pay for everything the same way."

The mother glares at her. "Yes," she says. "It is."

The saleswoman punches the keys on the register and the mother swipes her card and hands over the cash. The saleswoman gives her the bear and two receipts and the mother walks out with the kids, their faces alight as they sing some bear song I don't know.

"Let's do that," Keegan whispers. "Put fifteen dollars on my network card and spend whatever we want in cash."

"Okay."

"That way we can get her a bear, medium-sized, and a costume. Something nice."

"Okay," I say. "But not a princess dress."

"Fine."

We go back out to the parking lot, our budget blown twice over. Keegan carries a bag with a large bear wearing overalls and a T-shirt that says "Bear With Me." I tell myself this might be the bear that stays with Olivia all through her childhood, the bear she'll take on car rides and airplanes if Maria ever gets to take her anywhere.

"I could kind of use a drink."

"Me, too. Jesus. Scottsdale?"

"Deal. But nowhere southwestern."

"Deal."

We've tried to be poor and failed completely.

TEMPE, Ariz., Feb. 19 The grass at the park looks thick and green from a distance, but walking into it you see the gaps and dirt. The cracked ground is so hard I expect Olivia to cry every time she falls on her walk from Maria to me but instead she laughs. She's a beautiful kid, with big, maple-syrup-colored eyes like her mother's, and hair that's soft and thin like an old man's.

At first I won't even crouch down to play with her. I don't want Maria's family to think I'm auditioning to be her boyfriend or Olivia's dad. But I only need about twelve seconds to realize you can't be reserved with a one-year-old. They don't have boundaries. After a few minutes of pretending to have fun with Olivia I actually do.

"She's some kind of genius or something," I tell Maria. "I didn't know babies could walk this young."

Maria laughs, her tongue pink like a dolphin's. She looks even younger at the park than at work. "Yeah," she says. "She's a genius. Like her mom."

"Does she talk?"

"She talks all the time, but only to me. With her mind. She's like, tell this dude thanks for the awesome bear."

I laugh. Keegan and I had tied the bear with ribbons and put it in a gift bag filled with confetti. But when I got here and found Maria and Olivia at the picnic tables, Olivia was too distracted by the sight of her relatives hanging a piñata to pay attention to what I'd brought her. We could have gotten her the cheapest bear in the mall. Or no bear.

Maria's cousin Chewie—when he introduced himself I had to ask three times if it really was his name—comes over from hanging the piñata to ask if either of us wants a beer. He says we would need to drink by his car to keep Maria's mom from seeing, and we both say thanks, maybe later. He picks up Olivia and spins her around, then plants her on the grass and ambles off to his car, around the corner.

"My mom's kind of crazy religious," Maria says.

"It's cool," I say. For once I feel better not drinking. I've taken the calculated risk of hiding the flash deck in my back pocket today, which works only because my shorts are so baggy. For added security I'm wearing a Depeche Mode shirt that hangs well over the back—a leftover from my fat-kid days that I usually wear only to the gym. I've ended up looking almost like Chewie and Maria's other male cousins, who wear shorts or khakis even baggier than mine and white T-shirts. The female cousins wear similar clothes, but tighter, and big earrings and necklaces. Maria stands out in tight black jeans and the Chucks she wears to work and a ripped Gumby shirt that hangs off one olive shoulder.

Olivia falls again and there's a long baby pause like she could squeeze out a cry at any moment. Instead she belches and laughs a high-pitched laugh. Maria tickles her and we imitate the sound, trying to make her do it again. Then I see Frank and we stop making noises.

He walks across the grass with two boys and a woman who must be his wife. Maria looks where I'm looking and makes a face when she sees Frank's family.

"I had to invite him," she says. "He overheard me inviting you."

The Franks start waving, Frank like he's reconsidering whether he should be here, Mrs. Frank like she's at a campaign stop. She's taller than he is, and pretty in a mall-ish kind of way, more Scottsdale than Mills. Frank's boys are probably seven or eight, and the younger-looking one has a rat-tail haircut I can't believe Frank allowed.

Frank grimaces at Maria and glances down at Olivia as if deciding whether she's clean enough to touch. Mrs. Frank looks at me.

"Ohhhh," she says. "I just love Depeche Mode. 'Bizarre Love Triangle' is the *best*. From that Gap commercial."

I look to Maria to see if she'll accept the burden of explaining that "Bizarre Love Triangle" is a New Order song and that the song Mrs. Frank is thinking of is "Just Can't Get Enough." Maria's occupied with scooping up Olivia for Frank to inspect so I decide to let Mrs. Frank go on being wrong.

"Grace Acuña," she says, holding out her hand.

"Scott Thomas," I say, shaking it. "I'm one of Frank's employees."

"How nice," she says. "And Maria's your girlfriend?"

Maria makes a face that stings my insides.

"No," I say. "We just work together."

"Well," says Mrs. Frank—Grace—finally letting go of my hand. "Think it over. She's awfully *pretty*."

She twirls her hair and smiles as if to provide a visual representation of the word "pretty." I'm surprised that Frank was able to land someone so conventionally attractive but remember that conventional attractiveness isn't the most important thing.

"Can I get you guys something?" Maria says. "We haven't started barbecuing yet, but there's water, juice, horchata—"

"A beer?" Frank says. "I'll have a beer. Scott, you?" He looks at his wife. "Honey? You?"

Mrs. Frank and I shake our heads no.

"I'm driving," I say.

"So's Frank!" his wife says. She punctuates the joke with an open-mouth grin that feels like a command to laugh. I try to kick in a stingy chuckle.

"One beer?" Maria says. "I'll be right back." She hands Olivia to me.

"Maria's mom—" I cut myself off, making sure I have the right grip on Olivia. "Nevermind."

Rat-tail and his older brother run off toward a soccer game by the slides and Frank and his wife look at me like I'm supposed to explain the lay of the land. Getting here on time has given me privileged information, like which uncle is which and when we're eating. I don't feel like giving it up too easily.

"So," I say. "What are you guys up to?"

"The usual," Frank says.

I don't know what the usual is. Olivia feels warm in my hands and I hope she doesn't need a diaper change. I'm unclear on the propriety of changing someone else's baby, especially while wearing pervert glasses.

"Did you guys see the piñata?"

I gesture toward Maria's cousins, who are still struggling to hang some cardboard creature from a tree with branches that rise too sharply to hold the rope with ease. I can imagine the urban planners of 100 years ago selecting just this kind of tree to foil the good times of future Mexicans.

"Ohh," Mrs. Frank says, "it's Quarby! A Quarby piñata. Jason *loves* Quarby."

I look over at the kids. "Which one's Jason?" I say. "Is he . . . " I touch the base of my neck.

"No, Ryan has the tail," she says, glad that I noticed it. "Jason's the older one."

"Which one's Quarby?" Frank says.

Mrs. Frank looks annoyed. "You know," she says. "He's on that show. He's a DJ, and he lives in a cave, and he has adventures, underseas. And whenever you ask him something, he says—"

"How does he DJ underwater?"

"He DJs for fun, when he's dry." She looks at me for sympathy: See what I have to deal with? She strikes me as one of those people who plan to someday land a sitcom named after themselves, with their real-life family members played by actors. Olivia burps and I pat her on the back the way I saw Maria pat her before.

"So," I say. "When do they start talking?"

Frank looks confused.

"Kids?" his wife says. "Too soon. And then they never stop." She slaps Frank on the shoulder and he smiles apologetically.

"I'll be right back," I say. "I think Olivia's . . . um . . . be right back."

I carry her toward Maria's mom, who's sitting at one of the picnic tables next to the piñata. Maria's aunts and uncles stand around her, telling jokes in Spanish too fast for me to understand. They unwrap cornbread and guacamole and chips that I'm disappointed to see come from a store.

Maria introduced me to everyone when I first got here and helped me say basic hellos in Spanish. Without her standing next to me I feel tongue-tied. I find Maria's English-speaking cousin, Alejandra, the prettiest girl here after Maria, standing behind the tables by the barbecue.

She's a few years older than Maria but still younger than me and wears a necklace with an eagle on it that makes me worry she has a boyfriend in the Marines whom I'm afraid to ask about because it's possible he's being shot at as we speak.

"Hey," Alejandra says. She holds out her hands for Olivia and I hand her over.

"I couldn't tell if she needed changing."

Alejandra raises Olivia and sniffs her diaper. "I don't think so," she says.

"Maria's getting a beer for our boss," I say, hoping my explanation for holding Olivia doesn't sound too defensive.

Alejandra gives a quick nod and hands Olivia back. "She likes you," she says.

I palm Olivia's head, bouncing her as lightly as I can. "Who does?"

Alejandra tilts her head. "Olivia," she says. "You wanted me to say Maria."

I raise Olivia and sniff her diaper. This is my attempt at playing it cool. "What makes you say that?"

Alejandra holds out her hands to take Olivia back. "Come on," she says. "You should talk to Maria's mom."

We go over to her table. She's in her forties, a smaller, rounder Maria, except Maria always seems to be forcing herself to frown and her mom looks like someone too busy to worry. She calls in Spanish to the people laying out the food, and I get the sense she would be doing it all herself if they hadn't ordered her to relax. Alejandra sits down next to her so they're both facing me and Maria's mom takes Olivia. She and Alejandra talk in quick bursts of Spanish, their voices like fast-pumping accordions. Finally Alejandra looks at me.

"She wants to know how old you are," she says.

"Twenty-nine."

Maria's mom nods. She exchanges a look with Alejandra and says something that makes them both laugh.

"She says Maria needs an older guy, not like Olivia's dad."

My cheeks feel hot. "Is Olivia's dad coming?" I ask, the opposite of hopefully.

Alejandra doesn't bother translating my question. "We've never met him," she says. "Maria says she's better off raising Olivia by herself. He's some high-school boy."

Frank and Grace walk up behind the table, where only I see them, and just as Maria's mom says something in accordion-Spanish, Frank's face contorts, becoming more twisted as Alejandra translates.

"She says Maria thinks you're the only one at Gringo's who's not an asshole."

I pretend I haven't noticed Frank.

"Ha," I say, without actually laughing. "Everyone there is so great."

Alejandra arches a meticulously shaped eyebrow.

"She also wants to know if you're Maria's boyfriend."

I look at Frank and Grace, who also seem to be awaiting my answer. Grace mouths the word yes, like she's feeding me my line.

"Well," I say. "*Maria es muy sympatica.*"

Everyone groans. It's not even a good dodge. Before anyone can devise a follow-up Maria appears at Frank's side with a Bud Light. She raises a finger to her lips as she passes it to him, then points to her mom's back. Everything's cool as long as she doesn't turn around.

"Whoa, look who brought a beer!" Grace announces. "We better check for ID."

We all shoot her dirty looks and she throws up her hands, basking in the bad attention. I mouth the words "Maria's mom," but she just looks at me, clueless about what she's done wrong. Maria's mom, oblivious, shakes her head and rubs noses with Olivia.

Grace spends the rest of the afternoon trying to usurp Olivia as the center of attention. When we eat chicken tostadas she announces that they're almost as good as the ones at her parents' restaurant, which has just opened its fourth location and is finally cracking the Tucson market. I say I have to go to the bathroom and get up. When I'm about twenty feet from the table she calls after me: "Don't flood it this time."

I feel a new sympathy for Frank, forced to live with this woman and her jokes, and the knowledge that her parents are more successful in the restaurant world than he is. I'm sure they would give Frank a job if he wanted one, but he's opted, somewhat heroically, to strike out on his own, to wake up every morning and arrive at work, often on time. Sure, he occasionally hits on a nineteen-year-old, and yes, he occasionally steals. But his home life explains a lot.

As I get to the bathrooms I see Jason and Ryan at the top of a slide. Jason has his brother in a headlock, and both seem likely to fall at any second. I intervene.

"Hey—Jason? Can you come down here for a second? Alone?"

He looks at me apprehensively. I wonder if he's frightened by the glasses. But then he releases his brother and slides down.

"So," I say to him. "I hear you like Quarby."

His mouth drops, as if he's stunned to be meeting the stupidest person in the world.

"Um, *yeah*," he says.

I stare at him. "Um, *yeah*? So that means you do?"

He looks confused. "I just said, didn't I? Um, *yeah*?"

This time he says it like a magical incantation that will make me smarter. At some point between the years of my childhood and the present day, sarcasm became our society's dominant form of humor, exposing millions of children to the "um, *yeah*" intonation years before they knew how to use it properly. "Jason," I say, "does your dad have any precision tools?"

He looks up at me, squeezing one eye nearly closed.

"Like a handsaw," I say.

He shakes his head.

"Okay. You can't cut things with a handsaw by just throwing it around, right? You have to use it carefully. And that's kind of how sarcasm is. If you throw it around, it loses its edge. Do you follow me?"

I notice his chin starting to shake. I could give up, just go to the bathroom, but he needs to hear this.

"When I asked about Quarby, you answered me like I'd asked something really stupid, as if it was a given that you liked Quarby. And the thing is, it's not a given. Many people have never even heard of Quarby. And to be honest, to me, he doesn't sound that cool. But I pretended to be interested because I was trying to make friends with you."

He looks at the ground, rubs his eyes. I'm worried he's going to cry and try to think of a way to wrap this up positively. "And I was just trying to make friends because you seem like a nice kid." And because he was about to kill himself and his brother. "So what would have been really nice is if you were nice to me back."

"Hey, guys. Having fun?"

I recognize Grace's voice behind me. I move to the side, afraid she'll put a hand on my back, and Jason looks past me to her.

"Um," he says tentatively. "Yeah."

I smile at him. The lesson has gotten through.

"Honey," Grace says. "You're doing it wrong. It isn't 'Um, yeah.' It's 'Um, *yeah*.' It's supposed to be funny, like when Quarby says it."

I suddenly understand. It's a catchphrase. Jason was trying to joke around with me. I try to convey my apologies with a look, then excuse myself again. As I walk off I hear Grace try to make Jason do the Quarby voice, but of course he's afraid to while I'm within earshot. I stay in the bathroom for five extra minutes out of shame.

When I get back to the picnic tables Frank is with Maria, trying to show Olivia how to hit the piñata with a plastic bat. Grace is at the table with Ryan on her lap, describing her family's spectacular success to one of Maria's cousins in the loud-and-slow dialect of English used by those who speak no other languages. Jason pleads with Frank to let him have a shot at the piñata but he shoos him away, saying the birthday girl gets to go first. Jason walks over to his mom, his fists clenched, but she's too busy with her story to pay attention to him.

I resolve to make up for my sarcasm speech.

Olivia drops the bat, teetering away from the tree, and I see my opening. Frank follows Olivia to the tables and I pick up the bat and ask Maria if we can give Jason a chance. She glances over at Frank and we share a conspiratorial smirk. Anything he doesn't want, we do.

Maria blindfolds Jason and spins him around. I use the rope to slowly raise and lower the Quarby, hoping Jason will knock its sarcastic ass to the moon. Before he gets the chance Frank comes back with Olivia and yanks the blindfold from Jason's eyes.

"What did I just tell you?" Frank says. "The birthday girl goes first. Is it your birthday? Are you a girl?"

So this is how it works at their house. Mom and dad dump on the older kid and he takes it out on his brother. Except now his brother isn't around.

Still holding the bat, Jason stomps past Olivia like he's going back to his mom. Frank tells him to bring back the bat and Jason stops, turns. He looks at Olivia, then Frank, then smiles. He swings the bat into Olivia's head.

The world goes silent as she hits the grass. Frank swoops down on Jason and grabs the bat as Maria falls on her knees and rolls Olivia face-up. Olivia's eyes are open but she still hasn't made a sound.

Aunts and uncles and cousins surround us and I tell everyone to stay back. I tell Maria not to move Olivia, that she might have a concussion. Her body is soft and slack on the grass, her hands balled up in fists.

"It's okay," Maria says, even though there's no evidence it is. Olivia has the red outline of the bat on her temple. Maria's mom falls to her knees next to her granddaughter, touching Olivia's shoulder as if touch might be enough.

"We need to take her to the hospital," I say.

"I'll drive," Frank says.

Maria's mom objects in Spanish and Maria translates. "No," she says. "You had a beer."

Grace interrupts. "It's not like one beer—"

Frank looks at her and she stops.

"Not now," he says. "Who else can drive?"

I start running for my car. Grace taunts Frank behind me.

"Look at the big manager managing," she says. "Mr. Fast Food."

I hate them both.

I wish I hadn't parked the Tomahawk so far up the street but I didn't want to blow my cover. I drive back to the park and hop the curb, speeding across the grass. When I pull up next to Maria and Olivia the family looks at me with a kind of awe, like I've landed in a spaceship. I leave the engine running and run around to open the passenger door.

Maria gets in first and her mother picks up Olivia, placing her delicately in Maria's arms. I run back to my side and reach across to buckle Maria in as her mom shuts the door. The family parts and I peel out. In the rearview I see Frank and Grace yelling at each other and their children.

Maria stares straight forward, her eyes watery and fixed on the Tomahawk's stained-wood dash.

"You bought this . . . with drugs?"

"It's, uh, my mom's."

She nods as if this conforms perfectly to her view of the world. We'll all be relying on our moms for the rest of our lives.

"For the emergency room," I say, "do you have insurance?"

She shakes her head, her eyes welling up. Olivia clutches Maria's finger, her big eyes vacant, like she has no idea how bad this could be.

"Maybe they'll just say she's okay," Maria whispers. "Maybe they'll just look at her, and say . . ."

So this is what it's like to be poor. I didn't get it until now. I thought poor people had some magical romantic ability to survive on nothing. But they don't. You can't get sick or hit with bat or do anything you haven't budgeted for. There's no room for bad luck. There's no room for anything.

"Forget it," I tell Maria. "I have a credit card."

She slumps in her seat and holds Olivia tight, not arguing because she can't. Arguing is for people with money.

TEMPE, Ariz., Feb. 20 Frank opens the drawer and slides the key across his desk. He crosses his hands and keeps his head bowed to look up at me. I stare at the key. This is supposed to fix things?

"I know," he says. "It's not much. If I could get you a raise for yesterday I would. But management would say it's too early."

He's completely blurring the lines. What happened yesterday had nothing to do with him being a boss. He's just a guy whose kid hit Maria's with a bat.

Of course, he's not the only one blurring lines. I stayed for eleven hours at the emergency room last night and still made it to work on time this morning. Frank called us exactly once at the hospital to see how Olivia was doing, but he was still forty-five minutes late getting here.

"Frank. What about the hospital bills?"

"I know," he says, shaking his head. "I can't believe she doesn't have insurance."

I want to climb across the desk and shove aside his coupon stacks, spit on him, hit him with a plastic bat, choke him with his manager tie. When they took Olivia behind the swinging hospital doors Maria lost it, crying for twenty minutes before she could even look at the forms. I held her and breathed into her hair. Her mom and Alejandra got there and nodded along with everything I said, like I was fluent in emergency and could translate for them the way Alejandra had for me. I gave my Visa to the woman at the window and told her to charge us whatever she had to when everything was done.

Maria's mom said no, and I told Alejandra it was just until we could think of something else. Maria's mom said okay, but she needed to know how much everything was to pay me back. When they called us behind the doors Olivia was on a gurney the size of a welcome mat under hot lights and I watched her big eyes stare up into the lamp like there was some explanation inside. They said they needed to give her an MRI and Alejandra asked me to ask how much it would cost and when they told me I told Alejandra to tell Maria's mom it was free. The doctor said he wanted Olivia to stay overnight for observation but that she seemed okay and that we were lucky the bat wasn't an inch higher, as if we weren't acting grateful enough.

When Frank called he babbled about "roughhousing" and "how kids are" and asked if Olivia was out of the hospital yet. I could hear his wife telling him what to say and ask. I said Olivia needed to stay overnight and he said, "Hmmmm" like maybe the hospital was making a mistake.

The police came and asked Maria how it had happened and if she was absolutely sure she had never gotten angry at Olivia and hit her, and she looked at them with red eyes and said of course not. They asked me if I was Olivia's father and Maria said Olivia's father was dead and they said, "dead?" And she said, "Basically," and they nodded like it was the right answer.

I look from the key to Frank. He exhales like he's wounded.

"I'll work something out with Maria," he says.

I feel my jaw tense. He'll work something out with Maria. He'll go from slipping her fives and tens to twenties and fifties, and by next Christmas he'll be back to asking her for crass little favors before he pays her, asking her to suck his candy cane or ride his sleigh or whatever cute shit he concocts, and she'll go along with it because he's her boss and she's young and poor and won't sue him like she should for the medical bills.

On Frank's monitors I can see Juan and Carlos prepping and singing. Bethany is giving someone at the drive-thru their change. Julio is cleaning the men's room and talking to himself. This is Frank's little kingdom. I've seen how he works things out.

"Anyway," he says, "thanks for what you did. I've been waiting for you to step up and take the kind of initiative you did yesterday, and, well, you've earned the key."

If I could argue with him without getting fired here or from my real job I would tell him that work and the park have nothing to do with each other and that rewarding me for something totally unrelated to my job is as illegal as trying to pay a subordinate for sexual favors. But I need a key so I just pick it up and walk out to the hallway, wondering why I consider either of my jobs worth keeping.

As I close the door I say, "Good thing my mom loaned me her car."

There's an icy pain in my chest as I realize the only thing that made me take the key was fear. Not of losing my job here or at the network, but of what I would do after, with no company policies to keep me from taking sides. The only excuse for neutrality would be cowardice. I walk out to the parking lot and dial Ann on my cell phone to tell her I'm paying Olivia's bills.

"Uh, no," she says.

"Why?"

"You know why."

I do know, but I want to hear her say it: paying a baby's medical bills would be a conflict of interest.

Because it would be pro-baby.

"I don't care," I say. "I'm doing it. The baby isn't a source. Her mother is."

"Scott," she says. Her voice is sharp, but she takes a breath and when she speaks again it's almost soothing. "Don't do anything yet. If you want to help these people, help them by finishing the story."

I breathe deep, remember that I like Ann, that she genuinely believes we're doing the right thing. In Ann's world the news is a tool for good and the story will do more to help poor people than I could do by helping a poor person. The fact that stopping Ferndekamp will also help our careers is supposed to be irrelevant.

Ann calls back after half an hour. I'm waxing the hallway outside Frank's office in the hopes that I'll be able to hear him if he calls Maria, or that my proximity will make him feel guilty if he doesn't. I lean the mop against the wall and walk back out to the lot.

"Okay," Ann says. "A very generous and very anonymous hotelier from Brussels has contacted the hospital and covered the bill."

She waits for me to thank her.

"Wow."

"But Scott. Next time you go to Brussels you'll be booking a very nice room at my aunt's hotel, just off the Bois de la Cambre. You'll have a lovely time, you'll sleep the sleep of angels, and Scott, you will pay through the nose."

She actually thinks I go to places like Brussels. She has no idea how idealized her view of life can be. I haven't taken a real vacation in two years.

"Thanks so much," I say.

At 9:30 the two cops from the hospital show up and look past me because I'm dressed like a fast-food worker. They go into Frank's office and the door closes, and when they come out they're laughing about "horseplay" as if their kids are always hitting people with bats, too.

Maria comes in at noon and tells me Olivia's okay, then disappears into Frank's office. She closes the door and I stand outside waxing the same spot for ten minutes but can't hear a word. When Maria comes out she says to follow her.

We go out behind the fence around the dumpsters, the one part of the parking lot Frank can't see on his monitors. I wish I could take the glasses off but there's no way I would be able to explain to Keegan why I did it. Maria puts her arms around my waist and falls into me and tells me someone paid the bill. She says she never would have known what to do without me and looks around to see if anyone's watching. I feel her small hands pressing into me and just when I think she's going to let go instead she stands up on her toes and kisses my chin.

It's the kind of kiss my mom used to give me before I fell asleep, a small, important kiss, the kind of kiss you give to tell someone I'm glad you're in the world.

But that's not how it will look to Keegan.

TEMPE, Ariz. Feb. 21 The high-school kids blast the rapper's duet with the country singer from their truck and the boys pour beer off the cliff in his memory. They try to lure the girls out of the cab to do shots of vodka and I want to tell the girls not to do it, that nothing good comes from drinking with high-school boys, but the last thing I need is for Keegan to see me talking to more teenage girls.

I caught her on her way out of her hotel room, her water bottle slung over her hip like a holster, her thighs tan and firm beneath her short-shorts. I asked if I could go running with her and she said only if I could be ready in five minutes.

The small talk has been bad—frequent flier miles are about to expire, the air sure is dry today—and as the trail got steeper we stopped talking altogether. Finally at the top of the mountain, while we catch our breath a few feet from the high-schoolers, I ask her how she gets the water bottle to stay on like that and she looks at me, annoyed.

"Why are you looking at my water bottle?"

She tugs at her shorts, trying to cover an extra inch of thigh.

"I don't know. Because we're . . . "

I stop. I don't know what we are. Keegan shakes her head.

"Scott, I'm sorry. I have to tell Ann."

"I wish you wouldn't. It was seriously nothing."

"You kissed a source, Scott."

I'm surprised by how hurt she sounds.

"I mean, God," she says. "You shouldn't even have gone to the party, much less told Ann you were going to pay the kid's hospital bill—"

"Don't."

"Scott, please. You've totally gone native."

She looks at me accusingly. She's put it out there. I'm supposed to get angry.

"It's not like I'm some cub covering a campaign who starts rooting for a candidate. And wasn't it my job to go native?"

She kicks a rock. "Not to mate with the natives."

"Please. Seriously. No offense, but I think I'm in a little more complicated spot than you are."

She smirks a mean smirk. I've made her feel defensive.

"What does that mean?" she says.

"It means it's really complicated to win people over and get them to tell you their secrets if they don't like you. It would be nice if we could just force these people to tell us everything they know but unfortunately they don't just spout quotes at our command."

She shakes her head and opens her mouth, then stops. She turns and runs down the trail and I run after her.

"Keegan?"

She's so far ahead I have to yell. Whatever she yells back is such a jumble that I'm halfway down the hill before I realize she's crying. I run faster to catch up, but she's really digging in, putting too much distance between us for me to make it up. I would have liked her so much more if I'd known she could run this fast, and so much less if I'd known she was running slower for me.

NEW YORK, Feb. 22 Ann stands at the door of the black box to make sure it tints completely. The room's been swept for bugs but Hanlon holds up a note pad on which he's written, "This is how I'll be talking today." Since the transcription debacle no one knows who to trust.

Ann sits down. When I told her about the song, she and Hanlon started having the transcription people followed home. After three days, one of them spotted his tail, and then they all stopped showing up for work. Ann said she and Hanlon would keep digging but that in the meantime we should press on with the investigation, that we had no idea if the transcribers were secretly working for the Evil Empire. For all we knew they had lined up low-paying jobs that had nothing to do with news and wanted to punish me before they left for my complaints about their shitty work.

Keegan is across from me, sitting between Ann and Hanlon like their good daughter. She's refused to look me in the eye since the run, and "accidentally" booked me in coach from Phoenix to JFK so she wouldn't have to sit next to me. I don't know what big gesture I could make to get her back since I never really had her to begin with. You can't tell someone you miss not being with them.

"You'll forgive me if I speak in a bit of coded language," Ann says. "But I've asked you all here because it's too important to risk over the phone. Our bird is about to sing."

Everyone moves in their seats. Rich, sitting next to me, clears his throat. I feel typecast by our proximity, guilty by association.

"I thought we were here to talk about the supposed incident with my co-worker," I say.

Keegan narrows her eyes. "Maria," she says. "Don't act like she's a stranger."

Ann touches the top of Keegan's hand, gently, like she's comforting some kind of victim.

"Sorry," Rich says. "But which one's our bird? I just came to hear everyone yell at Scott."

He taps the side of my shoe lightly with his to signal he's on my side. Great.

Hanlon scribbles furiously, then holds up his notepad to Rich and me. He's written "OUR BIRD."

He shows it to Ann, who nods approvingly.

"We'll talk about the Maria situation," she says. "But first we need to talk about the bird."

Hanlon opens one of his files and slides a photograph across the table to Ann. She holds it up to Rich. It's the old photograph of Carlotta Espinoza, waving goodbye to the guy in front of the Jetta with California plates.

"It turns out the guy she's waving to is her, uh, baby bird," Ann says. "We've tracked the location of the baby bird's nest using the, um . . . "

Hanlon scribbles and hold up his pad. It says "LICENSE."

"Right," Ann says. "Sorry, I don't really have a bird metaphor, since birds don't generally . . . "

Hanlon's already written "DRIVE." After he shows us each new page of scribble he tears it from the pad and tears it into little strips.

"Who's she planning to sing to?" Rich asks. "Or chirp to? Or whatever. I don't know what kind of bird she is. Isn't she really more of a cricket? Annoying but harmless?"

Hanlon scribbles, holds up the pad. "SHE'S A VERY DANGEROUS INSECT, WITH THE POTENTIAL TO DEVOUR, LOCUST-LIKE, OUR STORY JUST AS WE'RE APPROACHING HARVEST."

Rich looks at Ann. He says, "Harvest?"

"Yes," she says. She and Hanlon play the notepad game to communicate that Hanlon is getting a confirmation hearing by mid-March. We need to go to air by then.

"AND SCOTT'S DALLIANCES AREN'T HELPING," Hanlon writes.

"Sorry?" Keegan raises her hand, a completely brown-nosey thing to do since Ann is right there. She nods for Keegan to continue.

"I want to apologize for letting this get so out of hand," she says. "I'm not completely up to date on what Rich has, but with Scott having at least one . . . dalliance with a source, well. I just apologize for not reining in my reporter."

It's a cunning move. If she'd accused me of doing wrong there could be an explanation, a debate. But treating my supposed wrongdoing as established fact leaves me less room to maneuver. I have to play this carefully.

"Keegan," I say, "thank you." I smile at her, humbly, so she has no choice but to look in my direction and nod. She still doesn't look in my eyes. I look around the rest of the table.

"I appreciate Keegan's willingness to take the blame, but really," I say, "it's entirely on me."

Rich puts his foot on mine under the table and presses down like it's a brake. I hear him breathe in his lowest whisper the urgent syllables "u-ni-on." His way out of situations like this always involves calling his agent or our shop steward.

"What I'm saying is—" I look again at Keegan, who looks at me until she realizes what she's doing and looks away. "— that so much of our job is about being clear in what we intend to convey." I'm deliberately speaking in a halting, unsure voice, as if confessing.

"The truth is, I've watched the tape and I can see how it might kind of look like the girl, Maria—" I look at Keegan as if using the name is a huge concession. "I can see how prospective viewers could possibly misinterpret the images to think Maria did something inappropriate on or near my mouth. But I have to say that this was a definitely friendly, thankful kind of gesture and that I'm confident it doesn't represent any unfortunate feelings on Maria's part, which would obviously be unrequited."

Hanlon starts to write something, then rips it up.

"But to be honest," I say, "I think this is all something of a sideshow."

I try to remember where I've heard this phrase and realize with self-disgust that I've pilfered it from Rich. It's from his standard apology speech. I've heard it enough times to accidentally commit it to memory.

Keegan looks down, and Ann and Hanlon at each other.

Finally Ann speaks.

"You're right," she says, looking at me. She turns to Keegan to say, as an aside, "He is."

I feel my mouth open and close it.

"We need to finish this story," Ann says. "If we find out down the line that anyone has overstepped their bounds, we'll deal with that before going to air. But right now we don't know who's going to be in our story. This girl may not even be a sideshow. She may not be in the show at all."

Hanlon nods like a congregant trying to match his preacher's enthusiasm. Keegan looks at Ann and says, "Right" like she's not sure it is.

"And that show?" Ann says. "It's in two weeks. Three at most."

She looks at me. "And we're going to need something sexier than cleaning a bathroom without OT or international drive-thru ventriloquism. We need you to stop fucking around."

Hanlon holds up his notepad toward me. "NO KISSING, HUGGING, OR GIFTS," it says.

Rich chortles. "Sounds like a perfect relationship."

TEMPE, Ariz., Feb. 23 I leave a message on Harper's voicemail saying we really need to talk, that I hope she isn't still mad from last time and that things are more complicated than she might expect, that nothing is ever black-and-white no matter how much she wants it to be.

I tell her voicemail I know she has an incredible sense of right and wrong, that I really admire her for it, but that in my job there's a lot of grey area, that she shouldn't judge who I am by the things I do.

"I don't know," I say. "It goes back to the Batman thing. I mean, the suit is grey. Don't you think it's symbolic it's grey?"

I hang up and she calls back an hour later when I'm in the shower. I listen to her message on my voicemail.

"That is so . . . " she trails off. "The suit is *black*."

I call her back but she doesn't pick up so I leave another message. "It's black in the movies, Harper, which are totally dumbed down for the masses. In the comics it's grey. And you know that."

She doesn't call back.

TEMPE, Ariz., Feb. 25 The key opens Gringo's front door with minimal fumbling on my part and I whisper, "Thank you, Lord" and follow up my thanks with one of those vague and unenforceable prayers about trying to be a better person if only God would help me with this one thing. The one thing is for the key to work on Frank's office door as well as it did out front so I can steal his tapes and return them before the restaurant opens in three hours.

Keegan is across the street in the unmarked van with the local cameraman from before. Ann says Hanlon is checking on the fraud and trespassing issues of stealing the tapes but that we should at least find out if they have anything we want: shots of employee misconduct, stealing, whatever. I duck under the counter and it occurs to me that someday when all this is over I'll miss the morning bus rides and the smell of Lim Lam and the way a mop feels in my hands.

I go through the GRAND door and close it behind me so no one can see me from the street. I feel for the light switch and adjust my glasses on my nose. At least when I'm on to my next story I'll still have the option of watching almost every second I spent here.

I turn on the lights and my pants start vibrating with "Fight the Power." The call is from Keegan.

"Get out," she says. "There's a car in the parking lot."

"Cops?"

"No, just a car. Get out."

"I can't," I say. "There's no back exit."

"They're parking," she says. "Hide."

I hang up and set the phone on silent. I need to stop praying squirrelly prayers. I duck into the kitchen, holding my keys so they won't jingle, and crouch behind the fryer.

It's three a.m. on a Saturday morning. No one should be here, including me. I hear the front door open and close.

The phone says I have a text but I'm scared whoever's at the door will hear the sound if I press a button. On the other side of the GRAND door I hear people whispering and laughing. I hear a set of keys hit the counter. One of the voices says, "Why are we whispering?"

It's Frank.

"I don't know."

It's a woman's voice, shy. It should be Grace, but it doesn't sound like her.

"It's my restaurant," Frank says.

"Okay." The voice is almost docile. "Do you know . . . what time it is?"

"Don't worry," Frank says.

"I told my mom I'd be home."

The voice I so desperately want to be the voice of Grace can't possibly be hers.

"Look, if you don't want to—"

"I do," the voice says. "I just—what did you tell your wife?"

My phone goes off. I muffle the noise in my shirt and see Keegan's message: "FRANK AND MARIA."

Frank says something in a tone too low to hear.

"I thought she was staying with her parents," Maria says.

Frank goes low again and Maria whines a soft complaint he cuts off with "At least I'm here now." She complains again and he makes a series of low sounds that make her laugh like she's even younger than she is.

Everything goes quiet. I wish I could claw out through the floor. I hear my own breathing and feel my teeth chattering even though I'm not cold. I try to take deep breaths and then hear the metallic jingle of a belt opening.

"Thank you," Maria says. "For paying for the hospital."

"How could I not?" Frank says.

"I know you had to be anonymous," she says. "With your wife. But I want to say thank you."

I hear the belt-sound again. This is the thank you? He's worse than I thought. I want to get up and swing open the door, stop him before he accepts payment for something he didn't even do. Slay the monster.

But then they get loud.

Maria moans in a way that can't be misinterpreted. Frank makes sputtering grunts like he's chopping wood and something thuds steadily against the side of the counter. It creaks under her weight, or his, or both. I cover my ears to keep from hearing it but every few seconds I lift one hand to try to convince myself that it's not her saying, "Oh, my fucking God" or "Oh, daddy" or something in Spanish I don't understand. Frank doesn't use actual words except "Take it" and "You like that?" and something in English I don't understand. It goes on for maybe seven minutes before he cries out like someone is peeling back his skin. I hope maybe she is but then his sound turns into laughter and she laughs, too.

His next words are too low to hear, tender and repugnant, and her silence can only mean she has no idea how completely false they are, how nothing anyone says can mean anything when they're twenty years older than you are and you've just had sex on a counter under false pretenses. Why didn't Ann let me pay the bill?

They're quiet again for a few minutes and then I hear more deep sounds and finally heavy footsteps outside the GRAND door. Frank opens it and whistles Juan and Carlos' song, the one about too many women, and walks back to his office. I hear him turn the key and drawers open and close and then he goes back out to the front.

After he and Maria leave I text Keegan to make sure they've driven away and when she says they have, I go back to Frank's office. In his sex stupor he's left the door open but out of curiosity I try the key anyway to see if it works. It doesn't. I check Frank's shelves, the drawers, under the desk.

The tapes are gone.

I walk back to the van to give Keegan the bad news but she's leaning out the window, ecstatic.

"I got it," she says. "We didn't have time to set up a camera but I filmed them on my cell phone through the window. On the counter. Broadcast quality."

The driver gives me a thumbs-up. I get in the van.

"Also," Keegan says, "we're taking you to the airport. Ann needs you to go to San Francisco."

MESA, Ariz., Feb. 26 It's almost midnight by the time I find Carlotta Espinoza's house. I park across the street and reach into the back seat of the Tomahawk for the envelope. A last look at the photos inside: two men kissing over mimosas and omelets in the Castro District.

I put on the glasses and fanny pack. This is for posterity. There's no way we'll ever broadcast what I'm doing—no one wants to know how sausages are made—but Keegan and Ann and Hanlon will want to watch the tape for assurance I've done everything right.

As if anything about this is right.

I go to the door and knock. The Espinoza house has one of those "God Bless This Home" signs that always bother me. Why just this home? The private detectives Hanlon hired to follow Carlotta Espinoza reported she was a regular churchgoer, but we didn't know she was one of those people who think God is always paying specific attention to her.

This might actually work.

"Who is it?"

"Scott . . . Thomas," I call through the door. "I'm from . . . TV."

A girl of about sixteen opens the door. She's a miniature Carlotta, with the same round cheeks and narrow eyes.

"Why won't you guys leave my mom alone?" she says. "Your friend was just here."

"My friend?"

"The other TV guy," she says.

I can't begin to guess who she's talking about. Ann and Rich are in

Washington, getting ready for Ferndekamp's confirmation hearing. I just talked to Keegan at her hotel. Hanlon never goes outside.

"There must be some mistake," I say. "I don't have any friends."

She looks up at me, trying to decide whether I'm serious. Her face turns to pity as she decides I am. Then she sees the envelope in my hand.

"Let me guess," she says. "My brother?"

I look at her apologetically. "You're Mrs. Espinoza's daughter? Yvette?"

She shifts her jaw, not denying.

"Yes," I say. "Your brother."

We're doing one of the most evil things we've ever done, and one of the most embarrassingly unsophisticated. We tracked the California license plate on the Jetta belonging to Carlotta's son and cross-referenced the address with credit records. We found that he shares an address with another man in the Castro District. Ann said it was up to me, since I "know the Bay Area," to find out if they were roommates or more. She and Hanlon had hypothesized from Carlotta's church attendance that she might not want the world to know if her son were gay.

"It's none of your business," Yvette says. "He's living his life. Why should that be on the news?"

I try to look forlorn. "I agree. My network feels, unequivocally, that this is your brother's business. There's no way we're doing a story on it."

She nods slowly, suspiciously.

Smart girl.

"But we can't control what other people do," I say. "I mean, if your mom really wants to tell this courageous story about Ferndekamp, we're all ears. But whether she talks to us or someone else—really anyone else—we need to warn her that other news organizations might report things. About your brother."

This is how Ann told me to explain it. It lets us keep our white hats if what we're doing ever becomes public. We aren't trying to intimidate the Espinozas, just protect them.

Like the mob.

Ann and Hanlon didn't say it but I know they chose me for this ugly little job to test my resolve. Lately I've been thinking like a human instead of a reporter.

"Well, like I said," Yvette says, looking down at her family's welcome mat, "your friend already talked to her. She's been in her room crying and praying for like two hours."

I still don't know who my friend is supposed to be. Even if the network sent someone else to San Francisco, Carlotta's son and his boyfriend didn't go out together the entire time I watched their apartment yesterday. It was only this morning that I photographed the kiss.

"This friend of mine," I say. "What did he look like?"

She frowns, starts to close the door. "I promise," she says. "My mom won't testify against Mr. Ferndekamp. Just don't put my brother in the news."

"I won't," I say. "But can you tell me anything else about my friend? I need to make sure he doesn't put your brother on the news."

She closes the door and slides the chain, then reopens it a crack and peers out.

"He looked like you," she says. "But Mexican. With a ponytail."

"How is that like me?" I grip the door so she can't close it.

"Because," she says impatiently, "he had glasses like you."

My arm goes weak. I let go of the door.

"Was his name—"

She slams it closed as we say it together.

"Julio."

PHOENIX, Feb. 27 I wake up to the appley smell of Keegan's sheets and hear her at the door, thanking someone. I'm in her room. She let me sleep in her bed. I hear the door close and feel safe again, like things could turn out okay. Maybe despite everything she and I have formed a bond, an innate instinct to protect and care for each other rooted in something deeper than professional. Then I notice something heavy resting on top of me and jump out of bed. "What the fucking fuck?"

I stare down at the heavy thing, sprawled across the bed.

She let me sleep under a hotel comforter.

"Um," she says. "Good morning."

She puts a tray with a coffee pot and orange juice on the desk. She's wearing a bathrobe and her hair is piled on her head.

"A hotel comforter? Do you hate me?"

"It's almost six." She pours herself a cup of coffee. "You haven't missed anything. Ann hasn't called."

I came here straight from the Espinozas so we could call Ann together. It's strange that she hasn't called back, especially given the time zone difference with her in Washington.

"When did I fall asleep?"

"Around three. You were talking about how good a ponytail would be to hide a wire and how much sense it makes, in retrospect, that Julio would be so interested in your glasses. And how smart he was to put you on the defensive. And then you started mumbling about how his acne could have been makeup and you conked out."

I sit on the bed and brush off my clothes. "And you let me sleep under a hotel comforter."

She puts down her coffee and pours a glass of orange juice. "You fell asleep on top of the sheets," she says. "I slept under them. I didn't want you to be cold."

"But a hotel comforter? Haven't I told you about the germs? About all the stains you can only see under a blacklight? Is there anything dirtier in the world–"

"Look," she says. "You were shivering. I'm sorry. Do you want juice?"

She holds up the pitcher. I look at it, then at the comforter on the floor and finally back at her.

"Tell me you didn't know about Julio."

She tilts her head, quickly, like she's trying to decide if she heard me right. "I'm sorry?"

I lean forward. "You worked for the Evil Empire. I'm sure he does, too. Who else would try to swoop in and steal our story like this? If you didn't tip them off, who did?"

She puts down the juice and looks at me with her arms folded.

"Um, maybe our friends in the transcription department? The ones who tricked you with the song?"

I look at the floor. That would make the most sense.

"Maybe," I say, looking back at her. "Or maybe it was you."

She picks up her juice and sits at the foot of the bed.

"I'm not talking about this," she says, picking up the remote.

"Why? You have to admit it's possible. If you were in my position you wouldn't think it was possible? You wouldn't have the most basic newsperson skepticism?"

She turns on a show about dragons and sips her juice, ignoring me.

"Come on, Keegan."

She turns.

"I wouldn't accuse someone I had slept with any number of times of secretly spying on them for someone else," she says. "Because that would be unbelievably shitty."

I know I should stop talking but I can't. "Why would that be shitty?" I say. "That never happens? It's like every James Bond movie ever. The girl's always a double agent."

She turns back to the TV and turns up the volume. The dragons are talking about traveling to the end of the world.

"Keegan."

She keeps her eyes on the screen. "So you're James Bond in this analogy?"

"Oh, please. I ask a simple question and you make it like I have these—delusions of grandeur."

"No," she says, putting the dragons on mute. "No, you're totally right. The juice is poisoned. You've evaded my trap, Mr. Bond. Kudos."

I get up from the bed, look down at the comforter. "Is it that impossible?"

She switches to a financial station without answering. I go into the bathroom. My stomach is doing terrible things and I turn on the shower to keep her from hearing me. After about five minutes I hear her call out in the other room, "Oh, my God."

I flush the toilet and turn off the shower, then wash my hands as fast as I can. When I come out she's leaning into the TV, watching four guys in suits and a woman who looks like Kirsten Dunst throw around words like "mega-merger," "share price," and "obviously." Then the logos for our network and Gringo's appear on the screen with the caption "BREAK-ING: FAST FOOD NEWS."

"What's happening?"

Keegan goes to the fridge and pulls out two mini bottles of vodka, pouring them into her juice.

"We bought them," she says. She swigs and makes a face and swigs again.

"Bought who?"

She walks back to the bed and hits mute. She looks at me, wide-eyed.

"We bought Gringo's," she says. "The corporate conglomerate that owns our network has bought a controlling interest in Gringo's."

I go to the fridge and take out two more vodkas, then pour them into a glass of juice. The landline rings before I can drink and Keegan and I both dive across the bed to the nightstand to pick it up. She wins.

"Ann," she says into the phone. "We know. We saw."

I'm kneeling on the bed next to her to try to hear. She looks at me, invaded, and puts Ann on speakerphone, then slides away from me on the bed.

"I'm sorry not to call you back last night," Ann says. "I've been calling Wineglass, the bastard. He set this whole thing up."

"Okay," Keegan says. "What about the story?"

A pause from Ann.

"I guess I don't need to tell you it's on hold," she says. "They don't want us investigating our own acquisition."

I down half my screwdriver. So this is how it ends. I'm angry another story has led to nothing, angry all my months are wasted opportunities. But I'm relieved at the same time. I don't have to worry about Christmas Eve or what Julio has that I don't or what the story will do to Maria.

"Ann?" Keegan says. "What if we can do the story for someone else?"

WASHINGTON, D.C., Feb. 28 At the Starbucks in Dupont Circle I focus on the knee-level table to avoid meeting my co-workers' eyes. I think of the word *mesa*. Hanlon breaks my gaze by covering the tabletop with one document after another.

"These are Keegan's phone records," he says. "And a statement she swore out this morning. And a polygraph test she volunteered for afterward. I think it's clear to all of us she isn't a spy."

He glances toward her deferentially. Keegan sits between him and Ann with her legs crossed, wearing a plaid skirt and high-heeled boots to punish me. Her prized location befits her status as the only person who can save our story.

"Again," I say, "I was playing devil's advocate when I suggested—"

"It wasn't really a suggestion," Keegan says. "You directly asked if I was a spy. You said that since I'd worked for the so-called Evil Empire—"

Ann touches Keegan's shoulder. "It's okay," she says. "I wouldn't have hired you if there was any question about your loyalty."

I should have stayed in Arizona. I took the week off from Gringo's, telling Frank I got sick from some bad carne asada. After Keegan and I talked to Ann on the speakerphone, Keegan kicked me out of her room and called her old boss at the Evil Empire. It turns out that Julio does work for them, Keegan says, and that they did find out about the story from the transcribers. The good news—Keegan's phrase, not mine—is that they want us to join them. To quit our jobs and bring them the story our network is abandoning.

I try to imagine what that story will be and feel something like heart-burn. Keegan sips her skim latte as everyone looks to her to speak.

"My old bureau chief can put together offers today if we want them," she says. "They said their story would be even better with Ann's direction and Hanlon's counsel and Rich's secret source. They'd love to have you all aboard."

She looks at each of them in turn, building rapport and earning respect. Rich, seated to my left, claps my knee like he can't believe the good news.

"They'll also cover the costs if the network sues us for breaking our contracts," Keegan says. "But for the network to do that under the circumstances would be kind of Food Piggish."

She looks at me as if she's just remembered something.

"They say Julio got lots of good footage, and they were really excited about my shots of that little liaison on the counter," she says. "They couldn't use Scott's footage, obviously, since he filmed it with a network camera. But they said they'd love to use him as a consultant."

Everyone except me joins in a round of *Thank-you-Keegan*s and *I can't-believe-how-fast-you-did-this-Keegan*s and *Score-one-for-Keegan*s. I slump into my chair.

"Just to play devil's advocate one more time," I say. "Are they saying we've done enough reporting? Because I don't know if Julio has something amazing, but all your cell phone recording really shows is a manager and an employee having sex. We also know about the outsourcing and stealing from the register, but is the Evil Empire going to do a story on that? Because it seems like the kind of stuff we wouldn't consider . . . sexy enough."

I look at Rich, who looks at his nails.

"I guess what I'm asking is, would we be showing the counter footage because we think it reflects a systemic problem, or because we think it's sexy?"

Ann sips her cappuccino. "We realize," she says, "that you've become a little protective of the people you worked with at the restaurant. But we have to remember our obligation to viewers."

I take a sip from the Diet Coke I got at the corner liquor store. "Look, I'm not protecting anyone. I'm just trying to be fair. I don't know if some . . . dalliance between two people is enough to damn an entire restaurant, and I don't know if it's enough to bring down a cabinet nominee."

Rich clears his throat.

"Scott, it's not just two people. Ferndekamp is responsible for anything that goes on his restaurants, and he has to answer for it. There's a legal standard in these cases where someone can be found negligent not only for failing to correct things they know, but things they should have known."

I take a deep breath. Rich is forgetting that I explained this concept to him a year ago, when we did a story on wine for dogs.

I look at Hanlon, knowing it makes me seem desperate. "Couldn't people say we were only doing this story to play on people's basest instincts? I mean, isn't that the most obvious kind of propaganda, to show an older slug of a guy having sex with a girl most people would consider, you know, attractive?"

Everyone's quiet. Rich looks at Ann, who shrugs her shoulders, then does a two-fingered drum roll on his iced coffee.

"Scott, Maria isn't attractive," he says. "Maria is absolutely fucking *adorable*." He starts to cup his hands at his chest but catches himself. "Why do you think we picked that Gringo's in the first place?"

I look at Ann. A heartburn I've only vaguely noticed until now expands to my shoulders and lungs.

"Don't act like I've sold us out, Scott," Ann says. "You have no idea how hard it is to get the network to invest in a story like this."

Rich nods supportively.

"Rich's source had been to your Gringo's," she continues. "He went on and on about Maria. One Gringo's is as good as another, and why not go to the one with someone . . . photogenic? You know the stat. A news story is 81 percent more likely to go viral if the people involved are attractive. This could reach a YouTube audience that wouldn't normally care about cabinet nominations."

The pain constricts, contracts. What part of me hurts so much? My stomach? Intestines? Why don't I know more about my insides?

"We would have told you," Rich says. "But you didn't want to know. Remember when we said there were certain outliers? Irregularities?"

I remember. Everyone admired my integrity.

"One of the outliers was Maria," Rich says. "The other was Frank."

Human outliers. I turn back to Hanlon, who looks comatose.

"Remember what Hanlon said about census data? I'm not saying we should do that, but isn't there something to be said for empirical evidence?" I look around the table. "We know for a fact Gringo's outsources and pays shit. Why can't we focus on that? Why do we need to ruin these people's lives?"

Ann, sipping, nearly spit-takes. "I assume you're worried about Maria?" she says. "This is the life you're worried about ruining?"

My chest feels hot. Where does the esophagus end? What does the gallbladder do? "Okay, fine," I say. "Maria. Who knows how she'll end up looking in all this? We can say she's the victim, but someone will still say she's the one who accepted the money Frank stole."

Keegan answers, looking down at the table. "I think it's obvious to everyone you have . . . strong feelings," she says. "Maybe too strong."

Deep inside me Diet Coke pools at the bottom of my something.

"I didn't kiss her, Keegan. We've been through—"

Ann cuts me off. "Scott. You don't work for Maria. You don't even work for me. You work for the public. You owe it to them to be objective."

She pauses to make sure I get it. I don't say anything.

"The public has a right to see this story and see this footage and decide for themselves what happened," she says. "If they see a middle-aged man continuously harass and bribe a young single mother and see her finally have sex with him after-hours in a darkened fast-food restaurant, and if they don't think that constitutes harassment—well, fine. That's their right. But I doubt that's how they'll see it. And even if it is, the people have a right to know what's happening at a company owned by a prospective secretary of labor."

It sounds so simple when she says it. Which only makes it feel more wrong. Everything is turned around.

"We have to trust the viewers," Keegan says. "We're responsible to the public."

This is too much. My chest is burning. "Honestly," I say. "Can anybody here actually say they like the 'the public?' Because I really don't think you do. We keep dumbing these stories down, like if we get a hot enough girl people might watch and accidentally learn something, but I don't think that really happens."

Ann tries to cut me off. "Scott—"

"If we like them so much why do we treat them like such assholes? Why do we always have to do the stupidest version of every story possible?"

Ann's voice is hard, compressed. "We do the best we can to get our message out to the most inclusive audience possible—"

"Seriously, show of hands. Who here actually likes 'the public?'"

They look at each other, everyone waiting for someone else to respond. Ann looks around the Starbucks as if the members of the public themselves, chattering on their cell phones, might hang up and defend themselves. Rich's hand goes up first.

Keegan looks at him, then at the others. She raises her hand and shares a look with Rich: Of course she likes the public. Ann raises her hand next, as much to support Keegan as anything else. Hanlon's goes up last.

I focus on Keegan, shaking my head. "Oh, come on," I say. "I've been to malls with you."

She lowers her eyes. Everyone else looks confused.

"Here's the thing," I say. "Have any of you considered that Maria *is* the public? And that maybe the public doesn't like you as much as you like them? Maybe the public thinks you exploit people, that you treat them like idiots, and that your ethical debates always resolve themselves on whichever side is most convenient for you. Like in this case. Yesterday your new friends were the 'Evil Empire,' trying to screw us at every turn, but now you're jumping to work for them."

Everyone's hands go down. Keegan picks up her drink.

"If Maria's the public," she says, "have you considered that the public might not like you, either?"

We hear the muffled strains of "Margaritaville" and Rich digs into his pocket. He pulls out his BlackBerry and stops the music, then reads the message on the screen. He looks at me and puts the BlackBerry away.

"Okay," Ann says. "It's obvious Scott feels very strongly about his approach. Any decision he makes is his and any decision we make is ours. And we'll all respect each other's decisions."

I look at Keegan, her eyes brighter than ever.

"Is this about this," I ask her, "or is this about Maria?"

There seems to be a collective silent wince. I've gone there. No one knows about Keegan and me but maybe they've suspected.

"You tell me," she says.

"Come on," Ann says. "Let's do another show of hands. Okay. If you want to keep going on the story, with the deal Keegan's set up, raise your hand."

All hands go up except mine and Hanlon's. Ann turns to him.

"No," she says. "This is if you *do* want to do the story."

He finally stirs. "I know," he says. "Scott's won me over. It's not that I'm concerned about these people. I just don't think the story is very strong. And I don't know if this is the case I want to leave my job over."

I look down. Having Hanlon on my side makes me wonder if I'm in the right after all. Am I doing this because I really don't think we should do a story or because it's easier for me not to be involved?

Then I think about Maria. Having people watch her have sex on the Internet isn't going to help her. What she needs is college. She needs money and a new place to work, free from Frank.

"There's something you guys should know," I say. "I went into Gringo's on Christmas Eve. Which means our investigation started before New Year's. Which means Gringo's can sue us for fraud and the story is innately fucked."

Hanlon nods slowly, perhaps admiringly. I don't know if it's because

I'm trying to stop the story or because I seem to understand something legal. Ann stands up, followed by Keegan and Rich.

"I don't see how that matters," she says. "Now that you aren't part of the story."

She reaches past Keegan to shake hands with Hanlon. No hard feelings. Then she smiles at me.

"I'll miss you, Scott. But I'm glad you aren't doing anything you feel uncomfortable doing." She pats me on the shoulder. "And if you were in Gringo's before the first, it seems like this wouldn't have worked out anyway. I don't understand why you would do that."

Rich leans across to shake with Hanlon, then catches me off-guard with a long hug. Ann and Hanlon move toward the door. Rich lets go and starts after them, leaving Keegan and me alone.

Keegan holds out her hand and I take it without squeezing.

"Thanks," I say, "for being my hand-holder."

She pulls away, a flicker in her eyes I wasn't expecting. "Don't," she says.

I look one last time but the fireflies are dead.

She follows Ann outside, where they give Hanlon business cards he already has. When the network sues them I hope he won't be involved. Rich waits for me inside the door.

"Look," he says. "I get it. We all get it. That speech about the public, none of us take it personally. You have a thing for the girl. Who wouldn't? But at least keep in touch. The new network will probably let me drink. We'll go out sometime. We'll get *krunked*."

I nod. There are things about him I'll miss.

"Also," he says, "you have to see this."

He pulls out his BlackBerry and shows me the e-mail that set off "Margaritaville."

"It's a news release," he says. "Look who's listed as the contact person."

I see Harper's name and scroll down.

WHO: Animal advocacy groups

WHAT: Rally/Informational Campaign to protest inhumane foods sold at immigrants' rights rallies

WHEN: Wednesday, March 1, noon

WHERE: Runyon Canyon Park (Fuller Ave entrance), Los Angeles

WHY: While we respect and endorse the rights of undocumented workers to protest for fair treatment, we strongly urge them to respect the rights of another long-oppressed group: animals. Foods sold at recent immigration rallies in Los Angeles, Atlanta and Chicago have included *puercoperros* (hot dogs wrapped in bacon), *sapasitas* (stuffed cow tongue) and *sangre horchatas* (drinks made of rice and goat's blood).

We will be attending Wednesday's immigrants' rights demonstration, culminating at the south entrance of Runyon Canyon, and offering free samples of tofu tacos, seitan nachos, and regular, blood-free horchatas. The event will include caged, semi-nude women dressed as animals.

I pass the BlackBerry back to Rich, my hands shaking. He notices. "I know, right? *Naked chicks in cages.*"

LOS ANGELES, March 1 I run past pro-immigration demon-strators marching up the street with U.S. flags. Where the street dead-ends, at Runyon's front gate, a bunch of college-aged kids in canvas shoes stand a respectful distance from a taco truck, trying to intercept its customers with neatly wrapped burritos and tacos.

"*Gratis, gratis,*" they say, or "*sin animales.*"

Harper's people.

I pass through the entryway to the left of the gate, trying to find her before it turns twelve and the rally gets going. The pro- and anti-immi-gration demonstrators cluster on opposite sides of the paved path, near the green field where packs of actors and writers take free morning yoga classes. Farther up, near the trails into the hills, more of Harper's peo-ple cluster around open boxes of pre-made vegan food. Four women in bikini bottoms and body paint, each portraying a different animal, climb into cages. One of them presses herself against the bars from inside and I see two rows of stick-on udders lining her front, covering just enough to keep her legal.

In the middle of everything a reporter in spotless hiking boots stands interviewing a girl in a Neighborhoodie that says DARFUR across the chest instead of SILVERLAKE or BROOKLYN.

Harper.

I walk through the demonstration to get to her, listening to the two sides of the immigration debate chanting, "U-S-A," each side trying to out-do the other. The reporter plays with his earpiece, obviously annoyed that all these demonstrators keep demonstrating, and as he steps to the side I get my first look at her in months: smaller than I remembered, more cherubic, hopeful as ever.

The reporter leans in, male-coquettish, playing to the camera.

"So let me be sure I understand," he says. "You're in favor of the undocumented workers or against?"

The cameraman moves closer and I notice the network's logo. I lose some of my negligible respect for our local affiliates.

"Well, Nathan," Harper says to the reporter, "we aren't really protesting the protestors so much as protesting what they're eating. These immigrants want humane treatment, and we want that for them, too. But we also want it for all living beings, including animals. And as a new generation of Americans comes to this country, we thought, why not invite them to share in the best aspects of our country? Empathy, respect, and delicious, healthy food—"

"Wait, wait, wait." Nathan shoots a look to the cameraman: Cut. This was supposed to be simple.

Harper beams at him, wholesome, helpful. She always photographed beautifully, with the strangest-colored eyes. Nathan didn't pick her out of the crowd for what she has to say.

"Okay, wait," he says. "First, that was really long. Also: animals? What?"

She looks at the cameraman, sees the camera still lowered, and drops the smile. She turns to Nathan. "I'm not gonna bullshit you, okay? When we have demonstrations no one comes, so we're piggybacking on this one."

"By dressing as pigs." He gestures at the cages.

"One pig, yes. And a cow and a cat and a dog, to show that all kinds of animals are abused. So I'll make it short, and you can get some B-roll of some hot-yet-PG-rated ladies dressed like animals. Perfect, right?"

The cameraman raises his camera. Nathan smiles into it, starts over.

"So," he says. "You aren't against immigrants."

"No," Harper says, like the recipient of good-natured teasing. "We're against what they're eating."

Nathan leans in close. "But I know some in our audience are saying, 'Why shouldn't I eat Mexican food when it's so delicious?'"

She smiles back, pretending it's a great question, then ignores it. That's my girl.

"Studies have shown there are actually slightly higher rates of vegetarianism among Latinos," she says. "Not many people know this, but Cesar Chavez was a vegetarian—"

Nathan interrupts. "Who?"

"The founder of the United Farm Workers?"

Nathan is already scanning the crowd for a less talkative pretty girl. The cameraman tilts his head toward the cages, Nathan makes an excuse, and they disappear.

I cut Harper off from following. "Reporters aren't that smart, Harp. You really need to dumb things down."

She squints, shaking her head. "Glad you've been working on that cynicism."

I wait for her to laugh, the signal she's happy to see me. She doesn't.

"Are you covering this? Isn't that a conflict of interest?"

I roll my eyes, try for sympathy. "I'm pretty sure I'm getting fired soon. Or quitting. It's kind of ridiculous, I'm—"

She stops me. "Look, Scott, this is a *really* bad time. I have to talk to your esteemed colleague before he gets all his quotes from one of the strippers in the cages."

"Strippers?"

"From where you met me."

She walks off and I follow, slowly, hoping she might adjust to the idea of my being here. A man in traditional Native American garb starts dancing. Hikers come out of the hills with their dogs, looking confused. Actors and writers, lingering at the end of yoga, accept vegan burritos from Harper's team as Latino children light brown blocks and drop them on the pavement. The blocks spit red smoke, filling the air with a mildewy smell.

"Harper," I call after her. "Would it be the worst thing if he just got a quote from one of the strippers saying meat is murder? They're not as well-versed as you, fine, but it's not like he's gonna be able to follow anything complex. Even a sound bite is a great get in a story about something totally unrelated."

She stops, turns back to me. "Everything is related," she says, and walks into the smoke.

Police cars pull up to the gate. One of my many failures as a news professional is a total inability to estimate crowd size, but the one here must be in the hundreds. The guy from the taco truck does brisk business despite Harper's people and their fliers. I finally get to read one when a man eating carne asada drops it on the ground.

Conoce su carne, it says.

Meet your meat? Even I can tell the translation is off but it makes its point. There's a picture of a smiling pig beneath the lettering. A few of the yoga people nod approvingly when handed fliers, either out of agreement with the message or to pretend they read Spanish. A man dressed inexplicably in desert camouflage punches a man dressed inexplicably in a poncho covered in musical notes. The children light more bricks and Harper and I arrive at the cages in time to see four women in flats and business suits hanging the banner of their feminist group. They try to pass fliers through the cage bars to the women inside.

A cat-woman with painted-on stripes and whiskers recoils like a real cat, her fake ears seeming to arch.

"Please," the feminist says, "just read our flier. We like animals, too, but if you knew how people misinterpret this kind of protest—women aren't kittens or cows or dogs—"

Harper interjects. "Please," she says. "We're—I'm as much of a feminist as you are. I used to be a *stripper*."

Police crush through the gates. A burrito smacks the helmet of a riot-geared officer, who fires what must be tear gas. The smell in the air

turns from incense to fireworks. People rush for the meatless food, looking for ammunition against the officers and each other. Harper's people
circle the supply, joined by sympathizers from the yoga field. The cam-
ouflaged man breaks through the line and grabs an armful of tacos to the
cheers of his friends. A yoga practitioner scolds after him, "Dude, have
you even *heard* of *aparigraha?*"

Taco shells shatter all around. The cage doors open and the animal
women break for the gate. Harper chases down Nathan and I follow.
I just want a few minutes away from the crowd to talk to her alone, to
apologize for being so down on everything she's ever tried to do. But I
want her to say I was right sometimes, too: There's something to be said
for choosing your battles. Today should be proof of that.

Police pull out their clubs and stream into the red. Nathan crouches
by the gate and Harper, her hoodie gone, holds out her arms.

"Look," she tells him. "No one in my group threw anything at anyone. We're here for a peaceful informational campaign, we're not—"

He shakes his head. "Little late for that," he says. "Soon as my camera
guy gets back here, we're going live." He rehearses his opening: "Today
in Hollywood's Runyon Canyon, an animal rights group helps turns an
immigration protest—into a *food fight.*"

I come up behind her, taking her by the shoulders to turn her
around.

"Harp," I say, letting go, "Can I talk to this guy? I can drop some
names, slow him down. I saw the whole thing—"

She looks at me, blinking, smoke in her eyes. "I don't think so," she
says. "I wouldn't want you compromising your neutrality."

She turns back to Nathan. I hear a cop say, "turn it off" and then the
sound of a camera smashing to the ground. Nathan and I look up, then
at each other, and both of us run into the smoke. I find the cameraman
before he does, curled in a ball, wiping his eyes. "The salsa," he says. "It
burrrrrns—"

I find the tape intact in the wreckage of the camera and break it in half.
I find Harper again and hand it over. She looks at the tape, then at me.

"I was talking to him," she says. "We still could have gotten some of the message out. I was trying—"

"Uh-uh," I say. "You're way better with no story than the story he was gonna do."

She looks at me like there's only one thing left to say and I should already know what it is. "Simply because we were licked a hundred years before we started," she says, "is no reason for us not to try to win."

I have no idea what she's talking about.

"Is that from . . . Batman?"

She shakes her head, all her fears confirmed. "It's from *To Kill a Mockingbird*," she says, staring through me. "One of your all-time favorites?"

She puts finger-quotes around "all time favorites" so I'll know she knows I'm an asshole.

"Sometimes I just look at you," she says, "and I'm like, who is this person?"

I look down and see the taco shells at her feet: two of them, folded one inside the other, intact on the asphalt in the shape of a Gringo's heart.

She steps back, breaking it to pieces.

NEW YORK, March 14 Every day I worked at Gringo's I wondered how Ann and Rich were planning to assemble all our footage into something coherent. Nothing seemed shocking enough to bring down a cabinet nominee, even the fluid-in-food scandal that turned out to be nothing. But what they assemble for the Evil Empire is brilliant.

Keegan gets an on-air producer credit, and the surprising compassion within the piece shows how much she's learned from Ann. Rich, his hair and makeup unusually subtle, is an excellent viewer surrogate: skeptical at the start of the story but increasingly more appalled with each new revelation.

Julio ends up looking like a star, offering not only shots that are better composed than mine—he apparently never developed a fondness for Lim Lam—but also informed insights into the day-to-day life within Gringo's. I'm particularly impressed with his explanation of how Frank got away with stealing from the register: he used the coupons he stockpiled on his desk to offset all the money he gave to Maria.

Julio scores another showstopper with his emotional description of a fellow employee who was "forced to clean up fecal matter on unpaid overtime." The fellow employee, of course, was me.

Julio's most devastating material appears in a montage of scenes I could only have missed by not wanting to see them: Frank and Maria kissing by Frank's office, Frank passing her a handful of fives and tens from the register, Frank slipping his hands inside Maria's shirt. In the last shot he grabs her as she walks down the hall and presses her against a wall, kissing her hard. She slaps him, yells something about his wife, slaps him again. Then another kiss. Cut to another shot of him handing her fives and tens.

When the montage ends, Rich explains in a voiceover that Julio "acquired this exclusive footage during a daring six-week undercover investigation." Cut to Rich, in a polar bear tie, hugging Julio like he's finally back from the long ordeal. They share a hearty laugh, as if this is just another day in their long campaign to save the world, one restaurant at a time.

What sews the whole thing together is how well the Evil Empire illustrates the "never before revealed" allegations from Rich's secret source, who is never identified but gives off a human resources vibe. The source, shown only in shadows with his voice scrambled, explains that four sexual harassment complaints have been filed against Gringo's employee Frank Acuña in the last decade—and that each was quietly settled.

"And yet Gringo's continued to employ Mr. Acuña," Rich says, sounding stunned that this sort of thing occurs. "And not only to employ him, but to promote him, and eventually place him in charge of one of their flagship locations."

This assertion is backed up with hidden-camera footage of Ferndekamp himself, saying in a speech to Gringo's shareholders that he considers "each and every one of our restaurants a flagship." This is the only comment from Ferndekamp in the story, except for some shaky-cam footage of him getting out of a limousine and walking into the White House as Rich shouts, from behind a fence, "Why haven't you returned our calls?" and then, "What do you have to say to Maria?"

Ferndekamp, ambushed, looks directly into the camera and says, "Maria who?" as one of his handlers pulls him away.

As I'd feared, Maria is at the center of the story. Rich explains this in his intro, an accurate transcript of which is included in a news release sent by the Evil Empire to every other news agency in the country:

> **Tonight we bring you the story of a fast-food company that let one of its key managers take advantage of an unwed teenage mother—and run one of its franchises like his personal playhouse. He was allowed to treat his employees like servants—and,**

as our hidden camera footage will show, to make a veritable sex slave of that young, unwed mother in particular. Why should you care? Because the man who runs the company that let this happen could soon be in charge of labor practices across America.

At the broadcast's climax, after a warning to send children out of the room, Rich plays Keegan's parking lot footage of Frank and Maria. This is the first time I've seen it, and the surprised look on Maria's face when Frank ties her wrists with her studded belt is almost more than I can take. He unzips his pants and tugs at her jeans. The picture blurs but not enough. Fade out. After a punishingly long shot of pure silent blackness we cut back to a somber-looking Rich, who asks his secret source if what we've seen in this footage is the norm at Gringo's restaurants. The source says that without proper federal oversight this could become the norm at every workplace in the country.

Immediately after the broadcast, local stations tease their own follow-ups, including interviews with local fast-food workers ("Has anyone ever made sexual overtures to you at work?"). The *Times* writes a balanced, second-day story noting that it has been unable to confirm "key details of the report at the center of the controversy"—it's hard to immediately match a daring, six-week investigation—but that the story has "nonetheless dealt a serious setback to Mr. Ferndekamp's chances of confirmation." I'm re-reading the part about how Hanlon and I were too skittish to take part in the "controversial and groundbreaking broadcast"—our names are mercifully left out—when I get a call summoning me to meet with Wineglass.

I leave the temporary cubicle the network has given me at the edge of the newsroom and take the elevator to the top floor, looking forward to being fired. When I step off I see the view of Central Park, surely spectacular when rain isn't cascading down the sloping glass ceiling. I walk back to Wineglass's office, a larger version of the black box, and find him sitting alone. The walls become dark, though I don't know how, because his hands are folded at the center of his desk, his index fingers protruding steeple-like toward a bright and shiny object.

The ring.

NEW YORK, March 22 Both of our top stories tonight are about us. The nightly newscast has been on-air for fifty-one seconds and my earpiece is still full of what we call "room sound," which is the sound a room makes when nothing in it makes a sound. The lack of white noise leaves space for every breath, every rustle of paper, to travel from the microphone clipped to my tie to the monitors in the control room and inside my ear. The technicians need to kill the sound in the next two minutes and thirty-six seconds because that's when I go live.

It turns out Wineglass didn't know we were investigating Gringo's until the day he caught me on his slope. When he asked what I was working on I told him everything, assuming he already knew. He promised again to let me know if his gardeners happened across the ring. When I left he didn't even call Ann to complain.

What he did do was call the other network higher-ups. Before long they were talking about how Gringo's could help the conglomerate that owns us to move forward in its transition from "information and entertainment services" to "overall lifestyle branding." Wineglass helped work out the details of the deal from the comfort of his sculpture garden.

The deal he made me in his office was this: We're doing a rebuttal to the Evil Empire story one way or another. If I agreed to appear on camera for a quick Q&A, he would give me the ring in return. It wasn't the gardeners who found it, he said. It was the guy who cleans the teeth of his frozen animals. Somehow, he said, I had landed the ring in the mouth of his giraffe.

Our lead story tonight is that our real six o'clock anchor, who was supposed to be reporting tonight live from Baghdad, is at Ramstein Air Base being treated for wounds from sniper fire. The fact that some people at the network still do real reporting makes my segment feel all the more embarrassing.

Steve, the fill-in anchor, is normally the Saturday morning guy. He handles the real anchor's injury with the sensitivity and aplomb of the cartoon characters with whom he normally shares the air. His intro—"You may notice I'm talking to you in place of your normal anchor. Our lead story explains why"—makes the guys in the control room gasp. I hear them in my headset, trying to be positive and professional despite the nervousness about Steve, about the real anchor, about my Q&A.

The room sound in my earpiece hisses into nothing, like someone compressing a balloon. It's Prius-quiet now and my heart starts beating hard but my hands are cold instead of sweating, and when I hold them in front of my face they don't shake.

"Please don't do that," Hanlon says in my earpiece. He can see me in the stationary camera positioned in front of me but I can't see him. I asked them to put me in a room of my own, with no other people or distractions or video monitors where I might have to see images of Maria. I don't want them to keep me from saying what I'm planning to say.

I put my hands down in my lap, off-camera, and Hanlon sighs his thanks. He's in the control room, basking in the producer's credit he earned by being the only other person too ethical or too cowardly to leave the network for the Evil Empire.

"Just relax," he says. "Let's do some good."

What about this story he considers good I'm not sure. What we're doing is truthful, yes, but at least the Evil Empire's misrepresentations might help the world. Our truth can only aid the status quo. Rebutting a story that hurts Gringo's can only improve Ferndekamp's chances of confirmation.

"Hanlon," I say. "Did you find out if the FedEx guy has picked up?"

"Yes," he says. "Five minutes ago."

The deal with Wineglass stipulated that he would give me the ring when I arrived at the studio to do the interview, and that I couldn't leave afterwards. I agreed, on the condition that I be allowed to FedEx it immediately. I told him I wanted to get my money back from the Canadian company that sold it to me. He agreed, even seemed surprised I didn't ask for more.

I listen to Steve ramble about the sacrifices reporters in Iraq make every day and feel grateful when a new voice comes over my earpiece.

"Ready?"

It's one of the techs in the control room. I don't remember his name but he's too friendly and comforting to work in TV news. Whatever else our broadcasts do, they give jobs to people like him. People with actual skills.

"Ready," I say, giving the camera a thumbs-up.

Hanlon clears his throat. I lower my hand.

"Okay," the technician says. "We're coming to you after Iraq. There won't be any count. Steve will transition straight in."

I give a double thumbs-up right into the camera just to make Hanlon nervous. Steve's voice rumbles through my earpiece.

"And now," he says, "a story about another reporter who made an incredible sacrifice."

I realize with horror he's referring to me.

"Scott Thomas is with us here in New York."

I try to remember everything Rich told me about being on-air: Smile. Be clear. Use as few words as possible. Forget the network has been promoting this all day. Don't think of the people watching at home, in airports, in bars. Try to forget the tourists watching on the big screens in Times Square.

Hanlon hisses in my ear: "Say something."

"Yes," I say. "Hello."

Hanlon sighs and Steve rambles.

"For six weeks, Scott Thomas was embedded in a different way than the correspondents in Iraq," he says. "He was in a desert, yes, but not in a war zone. Scott Thomas has spent much of this year working day-in and day-out at a fast-food restaurant in Nevada. I mean Arizona."

I should have asked for a monitor. If I knew when the camera was cutting away from me I could use that time to throw up. Steve describes the Evil Empire story and what it's meant for Ferndekamp's chances. He uses words like "stunning" and "controversial." Finally he gets to the part where we're supposed to acknowledge our network's failures. Of course this is where he hands off to me.

"Now Scott," he says. "There are those who will say you're only talking to me now because Gringo's and this network are now under the same vast corporate umbrella."

"Right."

"And because we're trying to undo the damage done to us by a rival network, and because we have a significant financial stake in the economic viability of our corporate partner."

"Some people may say that, yes."

"And some of these same people are even saying that this case represents the absolute worst of the corporate mergers that have swept across this nation in recent years. These critics say, furthermore, that this ever-evolving shell game of companies trading names and governance boards has left no corporate entity in this nation accountable to anyone, from regulators to customers to viewers."

"Right," I say. "Sure."

"Scott, if I could please finish my question—"

"Sorry, of course."

"These same people, Scott, would even say that we're contributing to this problem by putting a kind of happy shine on the alleged misdeeds of our latest acquisition. That the interview we're now conducting represents a clear-cut example of a corporation using its news division as a kind of bludgeon to shore up its financial interests—"

"Who's saying this, exactly?"

"Scott, please. And these critics would also say that by appearing on-air with me today you yourself are failing to halt the gears of the vast money-making machine, a rapidly evolving apparatus that has come to operate itself, for the benefit of the very few—a perpetual-motion money machine, if you will, impervious to the harm it does to our individuality."

I stare into the camera. Money machine?

"Scott Thomas, your response."

I lean forward. "I don't know where to begin," I say. "If I can focus on the . . . issues immediately before us, the only reason I'm talking to you now is because the information I have is true, and it raises questions about one of the key contentions of the previous report. We think viewers have a right to know what we know."

I hear Steve take a sip of water. Hanlon says, "You're doing great."

"People can question our motivations for releasing this information, and I'm sure they will. What they can't question is the information itself."

I relax. This isn't so hard.

"And that information," Steve says, "could torpedo the claims of sexual harassment and neglect that form the basis of the other network's report that has so bedeviled Mr. Ferndekamp."

It's a sloppy transition. I pretend not to hear it.

"Anyway," I say, "this is what I've learned. The situation at Gringo's was more complicated than a typical sexual harassment case. This particular manager and the employee, Maria, had a relationship that I guess might not have been the purely predatory one portrayed by the other network."

Steve flies a little abruptly into skeptic mode, forgetting we're all fake friends here.

"A very serious claim, one sure to be hotly disputed."

"I guess so," I say. "But the Arizona Department of Health backs it up."

This is the point where the document we obtained two days ago from an unethical state clerk is supposed to flash across the screen. From the "ooohs" in the control room I can tell that it has.

"Tell me what we're seeing," Steve says.

"What you're seeing," I say, "is a certificate of live birth for Maria's daughter, Olivia."

"And Maria is the very attractive young lady who was allegedly being harassed."

I blink to keep myself from rolling my eyes on-air. "Right."

"And why are we looking at this document?"

It's the first decent lead-in he's given me, but I don't know how to respond. Something—pride, guilt, who knows—led Frank to lend his full name to Box No. 6 of Olivia's birth certificate.

He's her dad.

"Scott," Steve says, trying again. "What does this document mean?"

I'm surprised how hard it is to phrase an answer. It means Frank wasn't just paying Maria to keep quiet about harassment. It means he was paying for food and diapers. Granted, he was trying to help in the most selfish way possible, but that's Frank. I clear my throat.

"It means . . . ummmm."

It means their relationship was much too complicated for anyone outside of it to ever explain.

"This birth certificate," Steve says, trying again. "With the father's name? Can you tell us how this raises questions about the harassment claim?"

He still sounds calm, but he must know I'm panicking. I hear Hanlon curse. Another voice, the technician's, says it's twenty-five seconds to commercial.

"Scott. In our final seconds here. Can you tell our viewers what this document means?"

My throat feels dry. I don't know how to answer but I have to try. "It shows some kind of, you know," I say. "Some kind of valid relationship, with them having a child, and not some kind of . . . "

I think about what Rich told me about being on-air: Smile. Be clear. Use as few words as possible. Don't say "had a relationship with" when you can say "had sex with." And then I hear the whirr and the hiss of the camera, zooming in.

They're playing this up for drama.

I feel my smile tighten. And this is when I get it.

There is no machine, no massive apparatus powered by itself. Just human beings, fueled by each other.

"Scott?" Steve in my earpiece. "What does it mean?"

"It means they weren't just fucking."

The voices in my ear explode. It's the noise a room makes when everything in it makes a noise.

Steve hurries us to commercial.

"Thanks for that, Scott. We'll be right back."

Hanlon comes through the door first, ripping me out of my seat and demanding to know whether I sabotaged the broadcast on purpose. The kindly tech is in tears. Wineglass kicks open the door, screaming that I'm fired, that I'll never work in news again.

"You can't say fucking *fuck* on live TV," he says. "Do you know what the fucking FCC fines are for saying fuck? Five-hundred-fucking-fifty-thousand dollars!"

I can't stop smiling. I find the stairs, then walk out into Times Square, where tourists who saw me on the big screens point and whisper. A woman covers her daughter's ears as I pass. Then, from the front of the building, Wineglass pushes through the revolving doors, smiling wide. I can see he's finally remembered a way to hit me back.

"By the way," he says. "That ring I gave you? Totally fake. Made of cubic zirconium, based on the specs you gave me at my house. All but worthless. I couldn't believe my luck when you didn't ask to have it appraised. Sucker."

He disappears back into the building, and regret washes over me. Because I didn't send the ring back for a refund. I sent it to Maria, hoping she would sell it and start over and forgive me for being such a fake.

LOS ANGELES, March 23 The good thing about saying "fuck" on national television is that Harper calls me. I get the voicemail saying she saw the broadcast and to call her as soon as I'm home from the airport.

"Can we go to Runyon?" I ask. "I have to make some apologies."

She's quiet. I can almost hear her calculating how little there is to lose.

"Sure," she finally says. "Why not?"

It's dark by the time we reach the lookout. The hikers and dogs are gone and we have the view to ourselves. We watch the lines of lights below, cars moving over L.A.

"I threw your ring off a cliff like this," I say. "Not exactly like this, not as pretty. At this party full of assholes."

She looks more amused than anything else. "You hate everybody, don't you?"

I look back, surprised, then shift my eyes.

"If I hated everybody I wouldn't have gotten you a ring."

She looks at me with an empty smirk: Lame. I try again. "You saw the broadcast?"

She zips her jacket to her chin. "Seriously," she says. "Best work you've ever done."

The lights seem to move more slowly.

"I knew you wouldn't care about a diamond," I say. "I was trying to show you I could commit to something."

She blinks, turns her head. "Yeah," she says. "Well."

"I should have signed your petitions. You should be able to count on your boyfriend, your ex-boyfriend, to sign whatever you want."

She looks at me. Her eyes are wet. "It should be easier than getting strangers to sign outside Whole Foods."

Something moves in the brush. I find a rock and throw it a few feet down the cliff to scare the sound away, making sure I see where it lands. This would be a bad time to injure an animal.

"I'm sorry if I made you feel small," I say. "Like you weren't doing any good. At least you tried. I'm sorry I tried to make you someone not as good as you are."

She moves closer and puts an arm around me, burying her face in my shoulder. I feel her shake.

"Thanks," she says. "I appreciate it. I appreciate you saying it."

The shaking gets worse. The lights go faster.

"But Scott—you know it's too late, right?"

"I need it to be too late," I say. "So you'll know I mean it."

I've been afraid to touch her until now but I reach across to pull her closer. I feel something in her jacket, sharp and rectangular. She leans back to look at me and I think about losing her here, long before she left for Virginia.

"I wasn't really that into Batman," she says. "I got a comic from a Secret Santa in my department and you were so psyched I bought a couple more. But I read them and they were retarded."

"Too much grey area?"

She takes the book from her jacket and gives it to me. I flip through the pages.

"Thanks," I say. "I'm sure this will be better."

We watch the lights and listen to the canyon. Then I remember one last thing.

"I'm sorry I never congratulated you on winning your election."

BERKELEY, Calif., June 1 "So what do you do?"

The girl is slumming like nearly everyone in the bar, sitting next to me on a crooked stool with a ripped vinyl seat. Someone, one of her friends, keeps replaying "Heart of Gold" on the jukebox. I look at my whiskey, trying to catch the ice shifting as it melts, and decide to tell her the truth.

"I'm a day laborer."

Her face loses its softness. She brushes her bangs with a jangle of bracelets and stares at me. "That's in really bad taste," she says. "I don't know how much you know about migrant workers, but they're basically doing hard labor without health insurance or workers comp."

I look across the bar at the old cash register, trying to guess how long ago, if you took away the dialogue, all this could have taken place. I look back at her, half-smiling. "It's only in bad taste if I'm, like, a reporter posing as a day laborer."

She crinkles her nose, picks up her purse. "Have a good night," she says, and walks back to her friends.

I ride BART to the North Berkeley station and bike home. My legs burn up the hill and I wish I'd had more to drink at the bar, but thinking about how early I have to wake up, decide it's best that I didn't. When I come through the door my parents are having dinner with the Alonzos.

Nestor gives me a redundant nod. Since this morning we've been apart only for the two hours I stopped at the bar. When I asked my mom if I could move home for a while she said the Alonzos were staying in my old room, that she hadn't found any loopholes to keep their landlord from kicking them out. I told her I could sleep on the downstairs couch. I didn't plan on staying long.

I mostly had the house to myself. Consuela cleaned houses during the day and went to school at night. Nestor did construction jobs he picked up in home-store parking lots. After a week I started applying for the kinds of jobs I'd missed out on when I joined the network right out of college: bartending, coffee houses, bookstores. Everyone laughed when they met me in person.

No one had seen me when I was on the news, of course. Barely anyone watched the news. But everyone had seen the thirty-second You-Tube clip of me cursing on the air. And everyone had clicked to the related video of Frank and Maria going at it on the Gringo's countertop. We were all famous in stupid ways. Prospective employers were sure I was only applying to spy on them. They turned into movie mobsters as soon as the interview started, making me pull up my shirt so they could check for wires.

After the second round of rejections, Nestor asked if I wanted to come to work with him. I laughed at first, not realizing he meant it.

We make twelve dollars an hour. Nestor started me off on demolition, hammering apart bathroom sinks and scraping up three-year-old tile. He showed me how to pour concrete, how to replace ceiling fans. I couldn't believe how much I didn't know. When contractors tried to talk to me in English I pretended not to understand.

Today we re-glazed floors and the smell of polyurethane made me want whiskey. I told Nestor I'd see him at home.

"You got some mail," my mom says. "A package."

I don't even go to the table. From the tone in her voice I know it's something I want to open now.

I find it by the door: a cushioned envelope with no return address. I peel back the forwarded mail stickers to see my name written in bouncy cursive over the address for the network apartment in Tempe. I rip open the envelope and a DVD clinks to the floor.

I start it on my mom's computer. The screen fills with sunlight breaking through stands of trees, shot through the passenger window of a car. I panic through a few clicks of static but the images return with a shot from outside the car: Olivia sitting in a car seat, gnawing on the foot of her birthday bear. The camera spins and settles on the car's roof, then auto-focuses on a cliff cropping out over acres of forest.

I try to guess where Maria got a car—her cousin? Frank is nowhere in sight. She rises into the shot, Olivia in her arms, their faces warm in the sun. She walks Olivia toward the cliff, holding her tight, then turns and holds out her left hand. A shaft of light hits the ring.

Maria walks back to the camera, sliding the ring from her hand to Olivia's, pressing all but Olivia's middle finger into a fist. She holds the finger up to the lens and the fake diamond fills the screen. She winks into the camera as if I of all people should get it and walks Olivia back to the cliff.

I understand, finally, that she doesn't know the diamond is fake. That she believes it could be the costliest thing anyone will ever give her.

She throws it over the trees.